Buddha at Bedtime

P9-CRU-869

Buddha at Bedtime

Tales of Love and Wisdom for You to Read
With Your Child to Enchant, Enlighten, and Inspire

Dharmachari Nagaraja

WATKINS PUBLISHING
LONDON

Buddha at Bedtime
Dharmachari Nagaraja

Distributed in the USA and Canada by
Sterling Publishing Co., Inc.
387 Park Avenue South
New York, NY 10016-8810

This edition first published in the UK and USA in 2008 by
Watkins Publishing Limited
Sixth Floor
75 Wells Street
London WIT 3QH

A member of Osprey Group

Copyright © Watkins Publishing Limited 2008
Text copyright © Dharmachari Nagaraja 2008
Commissioned artwork copyright © Watkins Publishing Limited 2008

The right of Dharmachari Nagaraja to be identified as the Author of this text has
been asserted in accordance with the Copyright, Designs and Patents Act of 1988.

All rights reserved. No part of this book may be reproduced in any form or by any
electronic or mechanical means, including information storage and retrieval systems,
without permission in writing from the publisher, except by a reviewer who may
quote brief passages in a review.

Managing Editor: Kelly Thompson
Editor: Ingrid Court-Jones
Editorial Assistant: Kirty Topiwala
Managing Designer: Suzanne Tuhrim
Commissioned Artwork: Sharon Tancredi (www.sharontancredi.com)

ISBN: 978-1-84483-623-9

10 9

Typeset in Cantoria
Color reproduction by Colourscan, Singapore
Printed in Singapore by Imago

For information about custom editions, special sales, premium and corporate
purchases, please contact Sterling Special Sales Department at 800-805-5489
or specialsales@sterlingpub.com.

A NOTE ON GENDER
In the introductory and concluding sections of this book intended for parents,
"they" is used to refer to your child or children, to avoid burdening the reader
repeatedly with phrases such as "he or she".

Contents

About this Book 6

Who Was the Buddha? 8

What Is Buddhism? 10

Why We Need Buddhism Today 14

Tales That Teach 16

Firing the Imagination 20

The Magic of Meditation 22

Before You Begin 24

The Brave Little Parrot 26
(Anything is possible when you're moved by love and loyalty)

Two Ducks and a Turtle 32
(Think before you speak)

The Prince and Sticky Hair 36
(Words are mightier than weapons)

The Grateful Bull 42
(Show others the respect you'd wish to receive yourself)

The Elephant and the Dog 48
(Even the unlikeliest characters can become friends)

The Quails and the Hunter 54
(Teamwork gets the best results)

The Princesses and the Kingshuk Tree 58
(Don't jump to conclusions until you have the full picture)

The Desert Spring 64
(Keep going until you achieve your goal)

The Lazy Wood Gatherer 70
(Don't put off until tomorrow what you can do today)

The Naughty Little Rabbit 74
(Listen to those who know more than you)

The Small Bowl of Rice 78
(Generosity is its own reward)

The Prancing Peacock 84
(Don't let pride and vanity go to your head)

The Dirty Old Goblet 90
(Honesty is the best policy)

The Golden Goose 96
(Show gratitude when it's due)

The Kind and Wise Stag 102
(Forgive others even when they have wronged you)

The Mischievous Monkey 108
(Hurting others only results in your getting hurt yourself)

The Whatnot Fruit 114
(Fools rush in but wise people show caution)

The Lion and the Jackal 120
(Don't let your fears cloud your judgment)

The Prince with a Lot to Learn 126
(Everything comes to an end, so make every moment precious)

Goblin Island 130
(Look beyond the obvious to find the truth)

Learning to Meditate 134

Metta Meditation 136

Rainbow Meditation 138

Breathing Meditation 139

Index of Values and Issues 140

Note from the Author 144

About This Book

Through my radio broadcasting work, I have discovered that nothing captures listeners' attention or gets a response quite like a good story. It was this observation that gave me the idea of retelling some of the Jataka Tales – ancient narratives, which are believed to have been told by the Buddha himself. My aim was to make the tales more accessible, not just to Buddhists but to everyone – and particularly to children. The collection of twenty stories in this book is the result, and I hope that you enjoy sharing them with your child.

In today's world, most people are used to experiencing stories through media such as radio, film and TV. In contrast, through the tales in this book, I hope to offer you the opportunity to take on the active mantle of storyteller. By engaging with the tales and reading them aloud with or to your child, you can create a powerful intimacy and set sail together into a world of wonder and imagination – sharing sights, sounds and, indeed, many feelings along the way. The stories have been especially chosen so that they will offer both you and your child valuable insights into the wisdom of the Buddha, and they are told in a way that makes this wisdom both easy to understand and fun to explore and assimilate with your child.

The tales are aimed at children ranging from six to ten years of age. However, you are the best judge of when your child will benefit from them, as every child's rate of development varies. At the start of each story, there is a vibrant, full-page, colour illustration of a key scene from the tale, which helps to bring the action to life for your child so that they can associate with the settings, characters and events as you progress through the narrative. All the stories start in a similar way: your child is asked to relax, be still and listen carefully. This is to promote a focused yet tranquil state of mind in which they will be particularly receptive to listening, absorbing information, thinking creatively and allowing themselves to be transported into the tales. This state will also encourage them to drift off to sleep after being read to at bedtime.

The tales can simply be enjoyed as entertaining stories. However, each one also subtly conveys a host of valuable Buddhist lessons, from which the reader or listener can draw anything that seems relevant to them. And to help you, as a parent, an essential Buddhist value is highlighted at the end of each tale – as a starting point for further discussion with your child if you so wish. These messages provide words of advice on themes such as compassion, generosity and impermanence, all of which are listed in the "values and issues" index on pages 140–44.

Before you read the stories, it's best to read the book's introductory section. Pages 8–13, written for parents and children to read together, give background on the Buddha and his teachings; pages 14–23, aimed mainly at parents, discuss the needs of children and how the stories can address these needs; and pages 24–5 present a short relaxation exercise for you to do with your child before a reading session.

In the concluding section of the book (pages 134–9), you will find guidance on the benefits of gently introducing your child to the Buddhist practice of meditation, including three fun visualizations. I wish you and your child a pleasant and fruitful journey together.

Who Was the Buddha?

The Buddha was a spiritual teacher from ancient India and the founder of Buddhism. His real name was Siddharta Gautama, and accounts of his life and teachings were passed down by word of mouth until they appeared in writing around 400 years after his death.

Not much information is known about the life of the Buddha, and what little there is has, over the centuries, become mixed with myth. However, it is said that he was born a prince of the Sakya tribe of Nepal in around 566 BC. As a child, Siddharta was troubled by the very same thoughts and fears that we all have today. He was worried by topics such as, "Why do things change?", "Why do we grow older?" and "Why do people get sad?" In his late twenties, he is said to have realized that the wealth and luxury provided by his royal position could not bring him real happiness, so he left his home and family to look for the meaning of life and the key to contentment by living simply and trying out the teachings and philosophies of his day.

For six years he wandered from place to place, living plainly. He studied with great masters and learned how to meditate (see pages 22–3 and 134–7), but still he felt unhappy. Then, one day, he decided to sit in meditation underneath a great tree, called the bodhi tree, and stay there until he found the answers he sought. After many days of deep meditation, he experienced an amazing flash of insight during which he came to understand the cause and true nature of human "suffering", and how to prevent it: he became what is now known as "enlightened". In fact, the name Buddha is a title which comes from the Sanskrit word

budh, meaning "to understand", or "to be awakened".
Buddha can therefore be translated as "someone who
has awakened to the truth".

For the rest of his life, the Buddha travelled around
India teaching others the way to enlightenment, a journey
which came to be known as the *Dharma* (the Path). Gradually,
he gathered a group of followers, who became known as the *Sangha*
(the Community). One important aspect of Buddhist practice was
that the Buddha encouraged the Sangha to think for themselves. He
directed them not to follow his teachings just because he said so, but to
test them for themselves. And he taught people from all walks of life.

Although the Buddha died at the age of 80 in around 486 BC,
his teachings have lived on. His last words are said to have been:
"Impermanent are all created things. Strive on with awareness." And the
Buddha, Dharma and Sangha – known as the Three Jewels or Three
Refuges – are still at the heart of Buddhism today.

May all beings be well.
May all beings be happy.
May all beings be free from suffering.
TRADITIONAL BUDDHIST BLESSING

What Is Buddhism?

There are around 350 million Buddhists in the world today, including a growing number of Westerners. Buddhism gradually became popular in India during the fourth century BC before spreading slowly to other countries in the Far East: northward into Nepal, Bhutan, Tibet, China, Mongolia and Japan, and southward into Thailand, Myanmar, Vietnam, Laos and Indonesia.

Many different forms of Buddhism have developed in these places over the centuries, and they vary according to the culture and customs of each country. However, the Buddha's basic teachings remains the same wherever Buddhism is practised. The most important ideas include believing in non-violence, being understanding about and tolerant of differences and having a strong sense of compassion.

The Buddha taught that we have to understand the nature of life before we can improve our own lives and become happier, so he formulated **The Four Noble Truths.** These give guidelines for developing ourselves and encourage everyone to strive for enlightenment, a state he believed could be achieved by all human beings. They are:

1. Suffering (or struggling) is part of everyone's life
2. The cause of our suffering is our own greedy mind, which constantly wants "more" and "better"
3. Suffering can be overcome
4. We can overcome suffering by following the steps of The Eightfold Path

The Eightfold Path involves:

1. Developing a deep understanding of The Four Noble Truths to inspire us to engage with the rest of the Path
2. Making a commitment to self-improvement
3. Speaking in a kind and truthful manner
4. Developing "right action" through behaving with compassion toward others
5. Earning a living without harming any being
6. Banishing negative thoughts to conquer ignorance and desires
7. Encouraging wholesome thoughts, because all that we say and do arises from our thoughts
8. Developing and strengthening the depth of our concentration

Another set of training principles, known as **The Five Precepts**, encourages us to take more responsibility for our actions. They are:

1. I resolve not to take life
2. I resolve not to steal
3. I resolve not to mistreat others
4. I resolve not to tell lies
5. I resolve not to indulge in excess

As you will see when you read the stories in this book, a central theme of Buddhism is that every action we take, every word we say, and even every thought we have, has a consequence. They all affect not only other people but also ourselves. The Buddha called this notion *karma* – we reap what we sow. This means that we need to apply thought and make wise decisions in everything we say and do, because anything unkind will come back to us. And since Buddhists believe in rebirth – that we each live many lives – actions in one life are likely to affect what we can become in future lives, if not in this one. Buddhists know that if they act kindly and wisely, they will eventually become enlightened and reach *nirvana*, a state of perfect peace and happiness.

Another important core teaching in Buddhism is that we find the greatest happiness in life when we dedicate ourselves to becoming loving and compassionate – toward both ourselves and others. The Buddha called this love *metta*, or universal loving-kindness.

So, how do Buddhists put all these teachings into practice? Generally, daily routine for a Buddhist involves some kind of meditation (see pages 22–3 and 134–7) with the aim of bringing more peace and harmony not only into their own lives but also into the lives of others. Monks and nuns, who in Eastern Buddhism have shaved heads and wear robes, may spend most of their day in meditation – whether in temples or in front of shrines, both of which usually contain one or more statues of the Buddha. Buddhists bow and make offerings to these figures, not as an act of worship, as, say, a Roman Catholic prays in front of a statue or a picture of Jesus, but because his image reminds them of their true potential. However, there are also many Buddhists in both the East and West for whom Buddhism is simply about having a certain attitude to life. And it is this peaceful, compassionate, loving, wise and selfless attitude to life that this book encourages you to develop in your children.

THE SIX PERFECTIONS

When a Buddhist's heart and mind are fully inspired by *metta* (see left), they are said to be a *bodhisattva* – someone who delays their own enlightenment to help others to reach the same state. The bodhisattva follows the path of **The Six Perfections**, which are a set of positive qualities that we can all benefit from cultivating in our own lives. As with the other Buddhist teachings mentioned on pages 10–12, they are explained here to help you and your child to recognize them in the stories that follow.

1. *Dana*: the wish to give freely to everybody without exception for no reward
2. *Sila*: the development of ethical behaviour
3. *Ksanti*: the quality of patience and the ability to remain calm, particularly in troubled times
4. *Virya*: enthusiastic effort, which promotes the strength and diligence necessary to progress on the bodhisattva path
5. *Dhyana*: concentration or meditation, which involves developing the mental ability to stay focused in order to make our actions more effective
6. *Prajna*: wisdom, not only intellectual understanding, but also gaining a direct insight into the true nature of reality

Why We Need Buddhism Today

Modern life can, at times, be rife with stress – whether about work, relationships, money or a whole range of other matters. Fortunately, ancient Buddhist teachings can help us to deal with this stress by encouraging us to infuse our all-too-often hectic, goal-driven lives with more of a sense of peace, love and compassion.

And it's not just adults who suffer from stress and anxiety. Children, too, have to cope with all sorts of stressful issues from an early age these days – for example, peer pressure, academic expectations, bullying, family breakdown. This means that the wise words of the Buddha can be just as beneficial for them, encouraging them to have a positive approach to life's problems and helping them to find a calm place inside themselves whenever they need it – a safe inner refuge.

Buddhist principles can also help to prevent us and our children from falling into the modern trap of always "wanting more" – as if external "things" in themselves, whether toys, clothes or whatever else, are going to bring happiness. In contrast to such materialism, Buddhism teaches that children, like adults, will only develop into truly happy, well-rounded individuals by looking inward and recognizing the wonder of their own existence.

Another Buddhist tenet that is particularly relevant today is that we should be mindful of and appreciate every single, precious moment – as each is gone in the blink of an eye and no two are ever quite the same. This teaching not only encourages our children to focus on experiencing life to the full, but also helps them to accept the impermanence of all things, making it easier for them to understand changes that occur in their life – whether moving house, starting a new school, growing older or losing a loved one.

All the stories that follow teach us about positive Buddhist qualities that are desirable not only for Buddhists but for anyone who wants themselves and their children to live a happier, richer, more meaningful life. For example, The Small Bowl of Rice (pages 78–83) deals with generosity, while The Prancing Peacock (pages 84–89) teaches humility, and The Kind and Wise Stag (pages 102–7) offers a message of forgiveness.

Almost all the tales convey a sense of respect for the natural world, too – not only through the settings, from parched deserts to lush jungles, but also through the characters, such as a smiling sun (The Brave Little Parrot, pages 26–31) and a moon who chats with the stars (The Lion and the Jackal, pages 120–25). These features encourage your child to recognize the beauty of the natural world, in the hope that they will learn to live in peace and harmony with their surroundings.

"The wind has settled, the blossoms have fallen;
Birds sing, the mountains grow dark.
This is the wondrous power of Buddhism."
Ryokan (1758-1831)

Tales That Teach

Stories, or parables, have been used throughout the ages and across cultures to communicate all sorts of important messages. The Buddha, for example, recognized that storytelling was the perfect vehicle to communicate his teachings (see pages 10–13). So what is it that makes stories such useful educational tools? Firstly, their varied settings, characters and plots provide listeners with something much more interesting and enchanting than any bare facts or theoretical concepts ever could. Secondly, stories often offer something personal with which listeners can associate, not only making the information conveyed easier to assimilate and understand but also easier to remember. And thirdly, stories encourage listeners to conjure up pictures of the action in their own head and therefore to engage more actively with any underlying messages.

Children, in particular, tend to respond well to stories. In fact, there is no better way to engage and nurture a child's imagination and capacity for understanding complex issues than with the help of well-written stories. Reading the stories in this book to your children will transport them to all sorts of magical settings, full of lively characters, where they will learn many valuable lessons about themselves and the world around them without feeling in any way pressurized or patronized.

"For men of good understanding will readily enough catch the meaning of what is taught under the shape of a parable."

THE LOTUS SUTRA

READING AND RELAXATION

The ideal time to read the stories in this book to your child is at the end of the day – the passive act of listening helps them to settle down and prepare for sleep after the excitement of their daily activities. However, you can read the stories together *any* time that suits you. For example, a good time might be after your child has finished their homework, to mark the transition from work to play. Children thrive on routine, so try to start at the same time each day. To support this, it's important to create a relaxed atmosphere, perhaps by turning down the light and lowering your voice when you read. Don't rush. Allow plenty of time, and read with expression and enthusiasm.

Although the stories are educational, make sure that reading them never becomes an academic exercise to test your child's vocabulary or their comprehension skills. Just focus on enjoying the story and be open to discussing the content (perhaps in the light of shared experiences). Always be sure to finish on a calming, reassuring note so that their mind is not overstimulated at an inappropriate time, such as just prior to going to sleep.

The 20 tales that follow (see pages 26–133) have been chosen from the Jataka Tales, which are stories believed to have been originally told by the Buddha himself, to communicate the many lessons he learned on his journey toward enlightenment. However, all of them are unique retellings, adapted for modern children, covering the Buddhist teachings (see pages 10–13) that seem most relevant to a younger audience – in as palatable a way as possible. It is hoped that the stories will appeal to all parents – whether of any faith or none – who wish to teach their children how to live compassionately, responsibly and contentedly. Some of the tales, such as The Prince and Sticky Hair (pages 36–41) and The Elephant and the Dog (pages 48–53), follow traditional versions very closely; others, such as The Princesses and the Kingshuk Tree (pages 58–63) and The Whatnot Fruit (pages 114–119), digress a little further from their Jataka sources for maximum appeal to children today; while The Small Bowl of Rice (pages 78–83) and The Prince with a Lot to Learn (pages 126–9) are more loosely based on seeds of wisdom from traditional Jataka tales.

The stories include a lively cast of characters, such as a compassionate parrot, a kindly buffalo, a fearless prince, an ugly monster and many more. But unlike traditional fairy tales or children's stories, their purpose is not simply to amuse, entertain or distract, but to express and communicate fundamental Buddhist insights – for example, that honesty is the best policy (see The Dirty Old Goblet, pages 90–95). In addition, many of the tales include a healthy element of humour and mischief, which will help to engage your child's mind and imagination all the more.

DISCUSSING THE STORIES

Sharing bedtime stories with your child opens a line of communication between you – whether you are reading just for fun or as a learning experience. To get the most out of your reading session, it is a good idea to limit yourselves to one story at a time and to take some time to explore your child's understanding of it. A great way to do this is to encourage them to take the lead in unravelling the threads of meaning that they have found most significant or relevant to their own life. You can aid this process by asking questions, but make sure that you don't talk down to them. Making time to discuss the stories in this way can be an educational and rewarding experience for you both as the stories presented here can be understood on many levels. You can read them again and again, and with each new encounter your child may find a different insight.

Another benefit often resulting from discussing the stories is that your child is more likely to confide in you and talk about any worries or problems they might have. This will enable you to gain a better understanding of your child and to offer them support and advice.

Firing the Imagination

All the great teachers of antiquity, including the Buddha, have emphasized that whatever we believe, we can become. This underlines the importance of the imagination, the ultimate source of all creativity. Every significant achievement in the world's history, whether spiritual or material, has grown from a seed in someone's imagination.

Creating opportunities for your child to use their imagination encourages flexibility in their thinking, which enables them to generate ideas and helps them to realize that there is almost always more than one possible solution to any given problem. This ability to appreciate different perspectives will not only help your child to become better at problem-solving, but will also enhance their ability to improvise when faced with the many challenges of daily life.

Each time you read a story with or to your child you are encouraging them to use their imagination by building their own unique picture of the action. In so doing, you transport them away from any day-to-day concerns and into new, exciting adventures. As well as enjoying these journeys for what they are, your child may also want to return to such magical lands by themselves, and so develop their own reading habit. They may even feel inspired to draw or paint scenes from the tales (perhaps starting from the accompanying illustrations). They might wish to elaborate on the stories – for example, by describing what could happen next – or even make up their own narratives, whether about characters in this book or others that they invent themselves. Such activities provide children with a liberating means of self-expression, and satisfy their innate need to be creative.

THE POWER OF VISUALIZATION

Visualization is a simple and relaxing form of meditation which can be particularly appealing to children. In fact, children (like the rest of us) use their powers of visualization quite naturally in day-to-day life – for example, when they conjure up a mental picture of how a foreign town might look.

The stories in this book actively promote visualization by using a level of language that will start painting pictures for your child, but without featuring so many details that there is no room for individual interpretation. To check whether your child is able to visualize a scene – for example, the tropical beach in Goblin Island (see pages 130–33) – ask them to describe what they see in their mind's eye. If they seem to be having trouble, get them to close their eyes and ask some guided questions such as, "What colour is the sky?", "What can you see in the distance?" and "What are the different characters wearing?" To help to further develop their powers of imagination and concentration, try the visualization exercises on pages 136–9, written specifically for children. The more they practise these, the easier it will become for them to build up their own fantastic pictures of any stories that they come across in the future.

The Magic of Meditation

A tool available to anyone of any age and background, meditation has been practised by many cultures for thousands of years as a way to nurture the human spirit and to live life more calmly and clearly, and with increased awareness. The practice has always been central to Buddhism – the Buddha himself was said to have achieved enlightenment while meditating under a bodhi tree (see page 8).

Sometimes known as the "royal road" to personal development, meditation is a direct way of working with the mind in order to transform it. Today in the West, it has become recognized as a highly valuable technique to tap into stillness and reduce stress. However, more and more people are also discovering how it can help us to gain insights into our true selves and therefore to develop a sense of self-acceptance and grounded self-confidence – qualities that are fundamental to contentment and that it's important to develop as early in life as possible.

One of the best methods of meditating is to simply sit still and focus your attention for a period of time on your breathing or on an object, such as a flower, a leaf or another inspiring item or image. Meditation begins by stilling the body (see pages 24–5) and then works to calm the mind. In everyday life, your mind is like a choppy sea. As you meditate, you descend down into the quieter, stiller depths of the ocean (your being) and, afterward, when you return your attention to everyday life, you find that the water's surface (your mind) has become much calmer. By teaching your child how to meditate, you are helping them to connect with their inner calm, their innate creativity and the essence of who they really are.

Far from being an inaccessible spiritual activity, as many people still believe, meditation can be very simple and fun for children, as well as enhancing their self-understanding and self-acceptance. Nowadays, forms of the practice are even finding their way into some schools to help with behavioural problems, such as hyperactivity and aggression. Once your child has learned how to meditate (see pages 134–5), they will be able to access a safe, quiet space in their mind at any time they feel a need for calm amid chaos.

One of the easiest meditation techniques for children to learn is visualization (see page 21 and 136–9). Through creating vivid images in their mind's eye, a child can tap into their own potential, and into positive qualities, such as kindness and generosity. Visualization is particularly beneficial for children who have low self-esteem, as it can help them to imagine positive outcomes, which give them the confidence to interact better with others and make friends more easily and successfully.

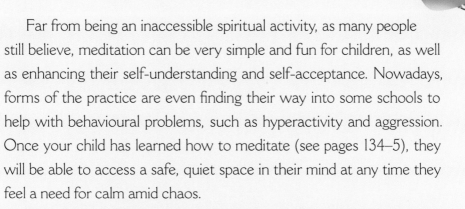

Just as the gentle rain falls from the heavens, fills the streams and rivers, and blends together in the vast ocean, so too may all the moments of your goodness pour out in one great flow to awaken and to heal us all.

TRADITIONAL BUDDHIST HEALING CHANT

Before You Begin

Before you begin to read the stories that follow with your child, it's worth spending a few minutes doing a simple stretching and relaxation exercise to bring both your child's and your own attention fully into the present. As well as helping to calm an agitated mind and/or body, the exercise will make it easier for both of you to concentrate on the story. And, of course, the exercise can also be highly enjoyable in itself.

Learning this simple technique also gives your child the tools to start releasing physical tension so that they can unwind and relax any time they feel stressed out or anxious. This means that they will know peace of mind is only ever a breath away.

Start by inviting your child to lie down either on their bed or on the floor with a pillow under their head. Sit comfortably beside them and ask them to gently turn their awareness to their breathing. Take a couple of deep breaths together – in and out. Then, when you are ready, say in a slow and relaxed voice:

"Close your eyes. Wiggle your toes … wiggle, wiggle … and relax. Now point your toes away from you … and pull your toes up toward you. Away from you, toward you … and relax.

Now, gently take a really big breath and imagine air filling your whole body, from your head down to your toes, as if you are blowing up like a balloon. Slowly let the breath out, little by little, letting your body sink right down into your bed or the floor.

Now, squeeze your hands into tight little balls ... and open them up,
stretching your fingers out wide. Squeeze your hands tightly again
and open them up, stretching your wide as you can ... and relax.

Take another really big breath in and imagine air filling your whole body,
from your head down to your toes, as if you are blowing up like
a balloon. Slowly let the breath out, little by little, allowing your
body to sink right down into the comfort of your bed or the floor.

Now, stretch your arms above your head and your feet, so that
you feel as long as possible ... and relax as much as you can.
Stretch again ... and relax. Stretch again ... and relax.

Now, bring your arms back down to your sides and place
your hands on your tummy. Scrunch up your face, so that
all your muscles tighten as much as possible ... and relax.
Now, give a big smile ... and relax all the muscles in
your face. Once more, smile ... and relax.

Breathe in slowly and deeply through your nose and feel your
tummy get bigger. Breathe out slowly through your mouth and
feel your tummy go lower. Relax, relax your whole body ...

Keep breathing deeply until you feel really relaxed, relaxed enough
to listen to and soak up the magical story you're about to be told."

The Brave Little Parrot

Relax, be very still and listen – listen carefully to this tale about a little blue parrot, who lived high up in the treetops of a tropical forest. One day, he surprised everyone, because, despite being only a small bird, he did a very brave thing. What do you think it was? Let's see if we can find out!

Now … one morning a big, dark storm cloud climbed high up into the sky above the forest where the little blue parrot lived. The storm cloud was very angry and he roared and thundered, making a terrible noise. He threw silver bolts of lightning down onto the forest, and one struck an old dead tree, which burst into flames. Next, the cloud took a big, bold breath and blew the flames, making sparks jump into the surrounding trees, which then caught fire themselves. When the flames reached so high that they were licking at the bottom of the parrot's nest, the parrot had no choice but to fly, higher and higher into the air.

As the storm growled and the flames grew, the little blue parrot looked down and saw lots of his friends – the other animals who lived in the forest – running around, confused and frightened by the fire. They didn't know where to go to find safety.

The parrot was worried about them, but stayed calm and tried to think of a way to help. Then it came to him. "Head toward the river!" he shouted. "Follow me, I'll show you. This way, my friends!" And he flew in the direction of the river to guide them. But not all the animals were able to follow – some couldn't hear him and others were trapped by the flames, crying out for help.

Suddenly, the little blue parrot had another idea! He flew down to the river and dived into the water, soaking his wings. Then, he flew back to the burning forest. When he was high above the flames, he shook his wings and little droplets of water fell down on the fire with a soft hissssss ... Back and forth he flew from the fire to the river, from the river to the fire. Each time, he carried feather-loads of water and sprinkled it on the flames.

The parrot was concentrating so much on trying to put out the fire that he didn't notice he was being watched.

High above in the sky, higher even than the storm clouds, floated a magnificent castle with gleaming spires and towers that shone as brightly as the stars. Watching from the castle were the gods of the happy lands. They shook their heads in disbelief at the parrot's actions. "What *is* that little blue parrot trying to do?" they asked one another. "Does he think he can put out that great fire with a few droplets of water?"

"Fly away and save yourself!" the gods cried out to the little blue parrot.

But the parrot's heart was so full of love and loyalty for his friends that he ignored the gods' advice and kept flying back and forth to the river as quickly as he could.

One of the gods could bear it no longer and decided to try to help. In a whoosh, he transformed himself into a great bald eagle and flew toward the burning forest where the little parrot was zigzagging in and out of the flames. "My little friend, you can't put out this raging fire with just a few drops of water, it's hopeless. Please, fly away to safety!" he pleaded.

"With respect, great eagle," cried the little blue parrot, "can't you see that my friends are in danger? I love my friends and if *I* don't try to save them, who will?" He was getting tired now – the smoke from the fire was making him cough and his eyes were stinging, but he wouldn't give up. The fingers of flames stretched up, trying to scorch his beautiful blue feathers, and his little feet were getting hotter and hotter. "Ouch!" he squawked, as he flew higher to escape the flames. But still he refused to give up.

The godly eagle was so moved by the little blue parrot's bravery, determination and love for his fellow creatures that he suddenly began to cry. His silver teardrops rained down, and as they flowed, they streamed onto the forest fire and the poor trapped animals. "Hissss, hissss, hissss!" went the angry flames, as the eagle's tears of compassion gradually put them out one by one ... until, finally, the fire was completely out!

The little parrot couldn't believe it – all the animals were safe! He whooped with joy and turned somersaults in the sky. And the sun couldn't help laughing, as he watched. All the animals cheered, "Hooray! Hooray! The brave parrot has saved us! Thank you! Thank you!" The storm cloud then slunk away, over the horizon, and left the sun to dry the forest with his warm, glowing smile.

The great eagle flew back to his castle in the sky, turned himself into a god once more and watched fondly as the happy parrot celebrated with his friends in the forest. "Who would have thought that such a small bird could be so brave, so determined and hold so much love in his little heart?" he said to himself. "He deserves a reward, and I know just the thing."

And so the god raised his hand and pointed at the little blue parrot. As all the animals looked on in wonder, a jet of multi-coloured stars flew down to the small bird and there was a big puff of smoke. When it cleared, the little parrot was no longer blue – his tail feathers now shimmered in all the colours of the rainbow. And he sparkled and glittered under the kindly gaze of the sun.

Sometimes we can feel helpless when faced with a great challenge. A wise person knows that love and compassion can give them the courage to achieve things that they thought were impossible.

Two Ducks and a Turtle

Relax, be very still and listen – listen carefully to this tale about a turtle who lived in a very large pond full of cool, clear water. That is, until something very strange happened! What could it be? Let's see if we can find out!

Now... this turtle lived a long, long time ago in a faraway land that was very hot. For many years, he was quite content swimming lazily around the large pond, or basking in the sun on top of one of the big, rubbery, green lily pads that covered its surface. Sometimes, he would snap at a passing dragonfly, or try to catch a fat, juicy water beetle to eat.

All in all, life was good for the turtle. Until one summer – one scorching hot and dry summer – the rain stopped falling and the sun shone so fiercely that the cool, clear water in the pond began to dry up. Little by little the pond shrank. Every day it became drier and drier, smaller and smaller, until finally there was so little water left that the turtle decided he must take action to find a new home before it disappeared completely. But how on earth would he do this?

Early one morning, as the sun took hold of the bright blue sky, the turtle set off to look for help. Before long, he heard two ducks quacking loudly to each other as they flew overhead.

Quickly, the turtle called up to them, "Ducks! You ducks up there! Please help me! My home pond is drying up. Would you kindly take me to a new pond full of water?"

"But how can we do that?" replied the ducks. "We're flying in the air and you're down there on the ground."

Now, as it so happened, at that very moment the turtle tripped over a long, straight stick that lay across his path.

"What if you carry this stick between your beaks?" he shouted up. "Then I could hold on to the middle with my mouth and you could carry me to a new pond."

"That's a good idea," agreed the ducks, landing beside him. "But, if we do, you must promise us that you will not open your mouth."

And so it was agreed. The ducks placed the stick between them and with the turtle holding on with his mouth, they took off. The ducks carried the turtle across the sky toward a pond full of cool, clear water shimmering in the distance.

On the way, they flew over a field where some children were playing noisily. Hearing the flapping of the ducks' wings above them, the children looked up and burst out laughing at the strange sight that met their eyes.

"How ridiculous!" shouted a boy. "Two ducks carrying a turtle on a stick! Doesn't he look silly!"

Well … this made the turtle very angry. Even though he probably did look odd, there was a very good reason for it. In his rage, he shouted at the children, "You're the silly ones. You don't underst-aaaa-and!"

As he had opened his mouth to speak, the poor turtle lost his grip on the stick and tumbled down out of the sun-filled sky, crashing onto the grass with a thump.

"Ouch!" he shouted, rubbing his sore, bruised head. "If only I hadn't listened to those children. I'll think twice before angrily snapping at someone again."

All too often, we open our mouths in anger without thinking about what might happen next. A wise person thinks before they speak, and if they can't say something kind, they keep silent.

The Prince and Sticky Hair

Relax, be very still and listen – listen carefully to this tale about a young prince called Hector who discovered something very important about his own strength. Would you like to know what happened? Let's see if we can find out!

Now … it was a beautiful sunny afternoon when the boat carrying Prince Hector back from overseas came into harbour. And before the young prince left the vessel, the captain warned him, "Your Highness, while you have been away training to be a warrior, an evil monster called Sticky Hair has come to live in the forest, so I advise you not to take that route to the palace. Instead, go the long way home around the mountains."

"Thank you for your advice," replied Hector, "but I'll be fine. I want to get home before sunset. And I have my weapons if I need them." "After all", he thought, "I'm a trained warrior. I'm not afraid of a silly old monster." And the young prince strode boldly on, into the woods.

Just as Prince Hector was beginning to think that the monster didn't exist, he reached a clearing in the forest and there stood the most gigantic, ugly creature he had ever seen. The monster was as big as a house and completely covered in matted hair. He looked like a living, breathing – but very horrible – haystack! The creature had a huge head and he stared at the prince with eyes as big as dinner plates. Two big orange tusks stuck out of his enormous mouth and his teeth were green and revolting. His belly was big and round like a beach ball and covered in large pale orange spots.

"Grrrrrrrr!" roared Sticky Hair. "What do you think you are doing in *my* wood, little man? You look like a tasty morsel and I'm going to eat you for dinner!"

"Pah! I'm not frightened of you, you horrible old monster," replied Hector. "I'm a warrior. I can easily defeat you with my sword. I dare you to fight me."

Swiftly as the wind, the prince leapt forward and thrust his sword at the monster. But to his surprise, it just stuck in the creature's sticky hair.

So the prince left his sword there, quickly rolled out of the way, got to his feet and grabbed his bow. Ptwang! Ptwang! Ptwang! He shot arrow after arrow at the monster, but, like the sword, each one just became tangled in his sticky hair. The prince was astonished.

"Ha, ha, ha!" boomed Sticky Hair, "You're very funny, little man! You'll never beat me!" Then he shook himself from his ugly head down to his big smelly toes and all the prince's arrows dropped down to the ground.

Hector now had only his club left for protection, so he swung it at Sticky Hair with all his might, but it, too, became caught in the monster's hair and was pulled from the prince's strong grip. "I'm not defeated yet!" he shouted. "My weapons may be useless, but I'm young and strong, and I'll fight you with my fists," he cried, as he ran and leapt on the monster – and got firmly stuck!

Even now, as Prince Hector dangled from the creature's sticky hair, he continued to act fearlessly. So much so, that the monster started to wonder exactly what gave him such courage.

"Why are you not frightened of me, little man? I could gobble you up in a snap and a crack!" he threatened fiercely.

Still hanging from the monster's tangled hair, Hector was busy thinking about what to do next. All of a sudden, it came to him. He realized that he would have to use his brains to outwit the creature, instead of his weapons. So he shouted up to Sticky Hair, "I'll tell you why I'm not afraid of you! My skin is coated in poison, so if you eat me you'll die. I dare you to eat me!"

Sticky Hair didn't believe Hector at first, but the more the prince insisted, the more worried the monster became. "Hmm ... I'd like to eat him, but I can't risk getting poisoned," he muttered. Reluctantly, he pulled the prince from his matted coat and set him on the ground, unharmed.

"Well, fearless little man, you've convinced me you're telling the truth and I don't want to die, so I suppose I'll have to let you go," he said, grudgingly.

Hector was delighted. Not only had he outwitted the monster and saved his own life, but he had also learned an important lesson: that the most powerful defence had been inside him all along – his intelligence! Not his strength or his weapons!

Looking up into the monster's big eyes, the young prince said: "I'm very grateful to you, Sticky Hair – not just for releasing me, but also for teaching me that I don't have to fight to be brave, strong and clever. Would you like to know my secret? If you promise not to eat me, I'll tell you as a reward for sparing my life."

Surprised, Sticky Hair agreed. Although the monster had never been defeated until that day, he had always been frightened of people. In fact, he had only attacked people to stop *them* from attacking *him*. But now, the creature was eager to learn to be fearless, like Hector, so he let the young prince become his teacher and friend.

And the strangest thing happened: the more Sticky Hair learned how to use his brain, the less he felt the need to harm others. Using his intelligence brought the creature great happiness and, gradually, he was transformed from a scary, lonely monster into a friendly forest giant.

Prince Hector let all the local people know that the "monster" had completely changed. And gradually they became his trusted friends, bringing him food and living with him in peace and harmony. And the new, eager-to-please Sticky Hair repaid their kindness by protecting them and guiding travellers safely through the forest.

Sometimes it feels like there's no option but to fight our way out of a difficult situation. A wise person knows that it's their intelligence, not their physical strength, that will help them to win in the end.

The Grateful Bull

Relax, be very still and listen – listen carefully to this tale about a big black bull called Delightful, who lived on Farmer Bruni's farm. Delightful was very grateful to the farmer who, despite not being very rich, took great care of him and all the other animals, and treated them with love and kindness. The grateful bull decided he wanted to do something to thank Farmer Bruni. Would you like to know what it was? Let's see if we can find out!

Now ... one evening, when Delightful was standing in his barn munching on some fresh hay after a long day working in the fields, he was struck with an idea of how he could repay the farmer. He did some of his best thinking when he was eating his hay at the end of the day.

"I'm the strongest bull on the farm. So perhaps I could use my *strength* to help Farmer Bruni? We could hold a contest against Farmer Chang's bull, Amos."

So, the next morning as Delightful was trotting out to the fields to work, he said to the farmer, "You are always so kind to me, and I've been thinking of a way to repay you. I'd like to challenge our wealthy neighbour's strongest bull to a tug-of-war contest. And we could have a prize for the winner. I'm sure I could win it for you."

Farmer Bruni thought that this was a wonderful idea, especially as he might make some money from his rich neighbour. So that afternoon he went to visit Farmer Chang, on the nearby farm.

"Good day, Farmer Chang," he said. "As there's not much work to do in the fields at the moment, I've an idea to liven things up". And he suggested the contest.

"What a splendid idea!" said his neighbour, "A tug-of-war between our strongest bulls would be very entertaining. But we'll need a good prize to make it worthwhile," said greedy Farmer Chang, as he imagined Amos beating Delightful. "I know. Whoever loses has to give a hundred gold pieces to the winner." And although a hundred gold pieces was a lot of money to Farmer Bruni, he was so sure that Delightful would win that he agreed to the prize.

News of the contest spread far and wide, and many local farmers gathered to watch. The two big bulls, Delightful and Amos, stood in the middle of a field with a rope stretched between them, tied to their harnesses. Farmer Bruni held his arm in the air and said to the bulls, "When I lower my arm on the count of three, I want you both to pull as hard as you can."

"One, two, three, go!" he cried, and the bulls immediately began to pull. They pulled the rope taut, and heaved and strained. But neither of the bulls seemed to be able to tug the other more than a little way.

After a couple of minutes, Farmer Bruni thought to himself, "Delightful should be winning by now," and he began to worry that his bull was going to lose. Panicking, he picked up a stick from the ground and hit Delightful on his back. "Pull harder, you lazy bull!" he shouted, "Put your back into it or you'll lose!"

Delightful was so shocked and upset by the farmer's words and actions that he just stopped pulling and didn't try at all. "This was my idea to *help* the farmer," he thought,

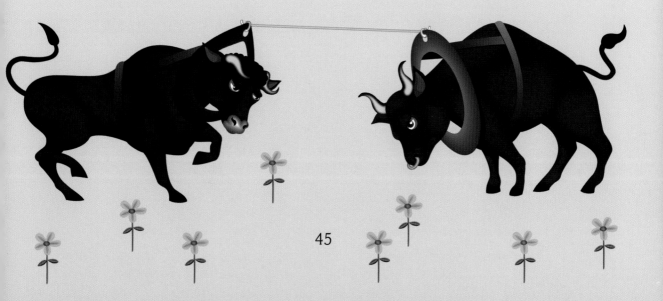

"I've never done anything bad to him, so why is he hitting and insulting me?"

Seeing his chance, the other bull pulled and pulled, and Delightful was dragged forward until Amos had won. Farmer Chang cheered and patted his bull, while the disappointed Farmer Bruni counted out the hundred gold pieces of prize money. Then, he went over to Delightful and shouted, "You gave up! You didn't even try, and now I've lost a hundred gold pieces! Are you trying to ruin me?"

Delightful shook his head and said sadly, "But you called me lazy, and you beat me with a stick. What have I done to deserve such treatment?"

This question shocked Farmer Bruni, and when he thought about what he had said and done, he realized that he had wronged Delightful. He hung his head in shame and said, "I'm so sorry. I panicked because I was frightened you would lose."

Delightful considered for a moment. He felt sorry for the farmer, "I understand. And I forgive you," he said. "We can still win. Go to Farmer Chang and suggest another contest with a bigger prize of two hundred gold pieces. But you must promise to be kind to me."

Full of admiration for Delightful's compassion, Farmer Bruni arranged with greedy Farmer Chang to hold another tug-of-war. This time, Farmer Bruni really encouraged Delightful. He cheered him on, calling, "Come on Delightful! You can do it, my strong, wise bull!" and he patted him on the back to show his affection and support.

Delightful pulled with all his might, moving backward step by step and groaning with the strain. Slowly and gradually, he pulled the exhausted Amos over the line to win. Farmer Bruni jumped with joy and hugged his kind bull. "Thank you for doing this for me. I'm so proud of you!" he exclaimed, while Farmer Chang stood frowning and looking shocked at having lost.

After Farmer Bruni had collected the prize money, the first thing he did was go and buy Delightful a cozy blanket to keep him warm at night. That evening they held a big party to celebrate their good fortune, and the farmer promised never to mistreat Delightful again.

It's all too easy to lose our patience with people and act unkindly. A wise person knows that showing kindness and compassion is the most effective way to bring out the best in others.

The Elephant and the Dog

Relax, be very still and listen – listen carefully to this tale about an elephant – a royal elephant, no less – who belonged to the king and had the privilege of leading all the king's processions. His name was Rajah and he lived in great luxury. But this didn't make up for his being the *only* royal elephant, which at times meant that he felt very lonely without anyone to keep him company – that is, until one day he made the most unlikely friend. Do you want to know who? Let's see if we can find out!

Now ... Rajah's evening routine consisted of having a long, cool bath before his keeper gave him dinner. Once he had eaten, he would pace around his compound and look at the sunset. Then, when the twinkling stars had arrived in the velvet night sky, he would go to bed.

However, one evening, when he had just finished his dinner, he noticed that he was being watched through the gate to his compound by a little white dog. The dog was skinny and had a hungry look about it.

"Mr Elephant, Sir," said the little dog, in a quiet voice, "I'm sorry to ask but please may I eat the food that you've left? I'm very hungry."

"Of course," said Rajah kindly.

So, the little dog crept under the gate and ran across to the elephant's food bowl to eat the leftovers. He ate them up in double-quick time, thanked the elephant and then scampered away into the night.

The same thing happened the next night, and the next, until one evening when the dog arrived, Rajah asked, "My friend, would you like to come and share my dinner every night? I live alone and would enjoy your company." The little dog was overjoyed and happily accepted this kind offer. What a strange sight they made: a huge great elephant sitting having his dinner with a little white dog!

Now, the elephant's keeper didn't think that the little dog was a very suitable companion for the royal elephant, so he did his best to shoo him away each night. But much to the elephant's delight, the little fellow kept coming back. And as the elephant keeper was a lazy man, he soon gave up and allowed him to stay. Before long, Rajah and Snowflake (as the elephant called him) were inseparable. When the elephant went for his evening bath, the dog would go with him and they would play together in the water. Afterward, they would have their dinner and then talk and talk, as friends do. And, of course, they laughed a lot, too. Then, when it was time for bed, Snowflake would curl up next to Rajah. It was a great friendship.

But then one day, as a farmer was returning home from his fields, he saw the two animals playing together and approached the elephant keeper saying, "That looks like a clever little dog. I would love to buy him. How much do you want for him?"

The elephant keeper saw this as the ideal opportunity not only to get rid of the little dog at last, but also to make himself some extra money, so he made a deal with the farmer, who took Snowflake straightaway.

With his friend gone, Rajah felt very lonely and sad. Little by little, he lost his appetite – he didn't feel like eating alone. In fact, he didn't really want to do anything much. He just stood looking over the fence in the direction that the little dog had been taken. When evening came and it was bath time, he refused to go in the water, and he didn't even notice the sunset or the stars as they shone in the clear night sky.

After a week of this strange behaviour, the elephant keeper started to get really worried about him. So he told the king about Rajah, who sent his very own doctor to have a look at him. The doctor carefully examined the elephant. "Well, I can find nothing wrong with him. He doesn't appear sick, he just seems very sad."

"Yes, he does," replied the keeper.

"Mmm, well people and animals don't usually get sad without good reason," said the doctor wisely. "Has anything happened recently? Have there been any changes in his life?"

"Not really … although he used to play every evening with a skinny little dog, who was bought recently by a local farmer."

"When did this occur?" asked the doctor.

"Oh, it must have been nearly a week ago, now," said the keeper sheepishly.

"And when did he go off his food and stop bathing?" asked the doctor.

"Uh … around about then, I suppose," said the keeper, feeling embarassed that he hadn't made the connection.

"Well, there you have it, he must be sad because he's missing his friend."

"Oh dear, I wish I hadn't been so quick to sell the little dog. I just thought they made such an odd pair! I'll try to find him but, to be honest, I don't know where the farmer lives," said the keeper feebly.

When the doctor reported this news back at the palace, the king sent word throughout his kingdom that a reward would be paid for the dog's return. On hearing of this, the farmer at once set out with the dog to claim his reward. And as soon as they entered the palace gates, Snowflake saw his friend, Rajah, and, barking with joy, ran over to him as fast as his short legs could carry him.

The elephant was overjoyed to see his little friend again. He picked him up with his long trunk, placed him on top of his head and marched off for his bath. That night, the two friends shared their dinner again and Rajah was happy once more. The next day, the elephant keeper had a special bowl made for Snowflake so that he knew he was welcome to stay for ever. And at the next court event, people marvelled at the little white dog who sat on the royal elephant's head at the front of the king's procession.

We all need friends with whom to share precious times and memories, and to help us in times of need. A wise person knows that they can find a friend among even the most unlikely of characters.

The Quails
and the Hunter

Relax, be very still and listen – listen carefully to this tale about a flock of quails, who lived happily in the leafy hedgerows and woods. That is, until one day, when a hunter came along. Do you want to know what happened? Let's see if we can find out!

Now … the hunter was a clever man, who made his living from catching quails. He would hide behind a hedgerow and imitate the quails' call, and they would answer him. When a good number of birds had gathered together nearby, he would throw a net over them to catch them. Then, he would take some home to his wife to cook and sell the rest at market for a good price.

The quails were led by a wise old bird called Tutt Tutt, who decided that something had to be done about the hunter. He realized that to protect his flock he would have to outsmart the hunter, so he devised a plan. One morning he called the quails together. "Every day the hunter lures more of us into his trap. Soon none of us

55

will be left. We must do something to protect ourselves. I have a plan. If we work together, we can escape him and his wicked net. The next time the hunter catches any of us, we must all fly up together from the ground when I give the call. That way, we'll be able to lift the net and get away. But for this plan to work, we *must* all co-operate." Everyone agreed that this was a great plan.

That very afternoon the hunter returned, hid by the hedgerow and imitated the quail's call. Once again, the birds fell for his trick, and he threw his net over them, as always. But this time, they knew what to do! As soon as they heard Tutt Tutt's signal, they all flapped their wings as hard as they could until they rose up into the air. The plan had worked! Their combined strength had lifted the net, which they then dropped into a large, prickly thorn bush.

The hunter didn't catch *one* quail that day. Each time he tried to capture the birds, they escaped and he ended up spending hours getting scratched and pricked while retrieving his net. When, finally, he gave up and went home, his wife was furious to see him arrive empty-handed. "Where are the quails for our dinner?" she snapped.

"Those birds outwitted me today – they worked together as a team," he replied angrily. "But they won't co-operate with each other for long. They're quarrelsome creatures and they'll soon fall out. Then they won't be able to lift my net anymore. That's when I'll catch them!"

Sure enough, one day soon, when the quails were singing in the hedgerow, one of them accidently sat on his neighbour's head and a big squabble broke out. Tutt Tutt begged them to resolve their dispute, but they wouldn't listen. Suddenly he saw the hunter, ready to pounce! Tutt Tutt realized that if the birds couldn't work together, then they would have to escape *before* the hunter cast his net. He told the flock to fly at once! Most of them rose immediately, but the quarrelsome quails were left behind – and were promptly caught. Tutt Tutt's flock continued to work as a team, outwitting the hunter so often that eventually he gave up trying to catch them.

It can be tempting to go our own way rather than to work together with others. A wise person knows that they can achieve much more as part of a team than on their own.

The Princesses and the Kingshuk Tree

Relax, be very still and listen – listen carefully to this tale about four princesses who lived in a grand palace in a distant land. They were very curious girls, so when they heard about a tree of breathtaking beauty, they longed to see it. But this was no ordinary tree – it was a magic tree. Do you want to know why? Let's see if we can find out!

Now … the young princesses had been well educated about everything in their own land – especially about all the animals, flowers and trees that could be found there. They even had a zoo in the palace, with exotic birds and animals from all over the world. And the collection of trees and flowers in the palace gardens was said to be beyond compare. So the princesses were very surprised one day to hear the gardener mention a special tree in the palace grounds, known as the Kingshuk, as none of them had ever come across it. The princesses were so intrigued by what they heard that they were determined to see it. That very day, after their lessons, they went to find the gardener and asked him to take them to see this wonderful tree.

"It would be my pleasure, your Highnesses!" said the gardener. "But the Kingshuk Tree is a magic tree: people can only see it on their birthday. The rest of the time it is invisible. So I will only be able to take you one at a time, and you will each have to wait until your birthday."

The princesses agreed and decided that it was only right and proper for the eldest to go first.

And so it was that on the eldest princess's birthday, a bright spring morning, the gardener and the girl set out to find the Kingshuk Tree. After walking for a while, they came to the edge of the royal forest where the gardener said that it grew. The princess saw a tall, willowy tree standing apart, but the gardener could see nothing, so she knew that this was indeed the magical Kingshuk. She stood entranced by the beautiful tree: its small green leaves were unfurling like sparkling emeralds and the princess was filled with its joyful energy. As they left, the gardener asked her not to talk about what had happened so that she wouldn't spoil the tree's magic for her sisters.

60

As spring rolled into summer, the second eldest princess celebrated her birthday and the gardener took her to find the Kingshuk Tree. She gasped when she saw it, for it was an explosion of deep-red blossoms, glowing like rubies. The princess swooned as she smelled the heavenly perfume of the magic flowers, which filled her with a great sense of happiness. The gardener asked her, too, not to discuss the tree until all the girls had seen it.

The hot summer days were turning to autumn when the gardener brought the third princess to see the Kingshuk Tree on her birthday. Her eyes widened when she saw its boughs crammed with luscious purple fruits, which hung from the tree like giant amethysts. The magic tree was so enticing that she felt as if it were feeding her with its goodness and generosity. And once again, the gardener asked her, like her sisters, not to talk about the tree until all four princesses had seen it.

Finally, as winter chased the last autumn leaves from the trees, the birthday of the fourth and youngest princess arrived. Now the gardener took her, too, to visit the Kingshuk Tree. She asked to be taken at night as she wanted to see it in the moonlight. And, sure enough, its silvery branches, wet with dew, looked spectacular and sparkled as if they were dressed in silver threads laced with tiny diamonds. She felt as if the mystical tree was wrapping her in its warmth and magic.

The day after the youngest princess's visit, the four girls went to thank the gardener for taking them all to see the magical Kingshuk Tree. Relieved that they could discuss it among themselves at last, the eldest princess said, "I will never forget that beautiful tree with its tiny leaves shimmering like emeralds in the afternoon sun."

"But, sister, you must be mistaken!" cried the second oldest Princess. "The Kingshuk Tree was covered in huge ruby-red blossoms and its heady perfume filled me with great feelings of happiness."

"Oh no, sisters, you are both quite wrong," insisted the third Princess. "The Kingshuk Tree was heavy with luscious purple fruits, which sparkled like giant amethysts."

"Well, sisters, I think you must have seen different trees!" cried the youngest princess. "The Kingshuk's branches were covered in threads of glittering dew that enchanted me with their magic."

Had the sisters not been so well-mannered, there might have been an argument. But instead they simply wondered if they had seen four different trees.

The gardener laughed. "Your Highnesses," he said calmly, "you have indeed each seen the same Kingshuk Tree and experienced its magic. But it was dressed for the season of your birthday when each of you visited. To truly appreciate the tree, you need to visit in all the seasons – which is, of course, impossible because of its invisibility!"

The princesses laughed. They had forgotten that each of their birthdays fell in a different part of the year and that the tree changed with the seasons. No wonder it had looked different on each visit!

The girls also realized that the only way they would be able to discover more about the magical Kingshuk Tree was by listening to – and learning from – each other and anyone else who'd been lucky enough to see it.

What we first see may not always give us the whole picture. A wise person knows that to discover the truth about anything, they must learn from other people's insights as well as their own.

The Desert Spring

Relax, be very still and listen – listen carefully to this tale about a poor family who were travelling to a rich cousin's wedding in a beautiful temple, far away. Do you want to know what happened on the journey? Let's see if we can find out!

Now ... the family had made good progress so far, passing through many towns and villages in their little cart, but suddenly they arrived at the edge of a vast and ferociously hot desert. Worried, they asked the local people for advice on how to cross it. Everyone said the same thing – not to go anywhere near it in the daytime, but instead to cross it at night, when the hot sun was resting harmlessly in bed. "But how would we know where to go in the dark?" asked the father of the family.

"Navigate by the stars," replied the locals.

"That's all very well," he thought. "But I don't know much about the stars, we need to find someone who does, to guide us."

So he asked around and soon found a young man who was said to be one of the best navigators in the region.

That night, after darkness had fallen over the land and the sands had become cooler, the family set out on their journey. The navigator took over the reins of the bullock and sat tall and proud in the cart. Gazing up into the clear night sky, he read the stars and directed them eastward.

However, he had enjoyed a very large dinner, not to mention a huge cup of hot chocolate, before setting out, and these were making him feel very drowsy. Before long, the gentle rocking of the cart had soothed him into a deep slumber, without any of the passengers, who were also asleep, realizing what had happened. Of course, the bullock leading the cart couldn't read the stars, so, with the navigator sleeping, it wandered aimlessly – in completely the wrong direction. When the father awoke with the first light, he realized they were well and truly lost!

"Where are we?" exclaimed his wife, when she awoke. Surely we should have nearly crossed the desert by now? We're going to be late for the wedding!" When they saw that the navigator was sound asleep, they were very angry with him, but their anger soon turned to fear. "A whole day in the desert!" the children wailed. "We'll run out of

water! What are we going to do?" they cried.

The father took charge and tried to calm them down. "Don't worry," he said, "we'll find a way out of this."

Pacing back and forth, he thought and thought. Then, he sat down on the sands and gazed into the distance. There must be something he could do ... Suddenly, he noticed a tiny green plant growing in the sand beside a rock. "Aha! Something *does* grow here in these hot, dry sands, after all. And where there are plants, there must be at least a little water!" he concluded.

He called the young, fit navigator over and showed him the plant. "I want you to dig here, as I think there must be water nearby," he instructed.

The navigator looked at him doubtfully, but as he had got them into this trouble, he was in no position to argue so he got a spade from the cart and started digging.

He dug and he dug – hour after hour. The hole became deeper and deeper, but still there was no water. The navigator was now very hot and thirsty. Suddenly, he hit something:

"We've hit a rock!" he cried. "All I've found is an enormous, dry boulder. What a waste of time!"

The rest of the family looked very disheartened. But the father of the family was not a man to give up easily, so urged them not to lose hope. "Don't give up now. We can't! If we give up now, we will all be lost. While we still have energy, and before it gets any hotter, we must keep trying. Think how our cousin will feel if we don't turn up for her wedding."

A silence fell over everyone. They all felt so tired and thirsty that they didn't even have the energy to protest. The head of the family sat on the rock and looked around. Then, in the silence, he heard or, at least, thought he heard, the faint sound of running water. "Am I hearing things?" he wondered.

"Listen carefully! I'm sure I can hear water! Can you hear it, too?" he asked.

"What? Has the heat gone to your head and made you crazy?" snapped his wife.

"No listen, I'm *sure* I can hear water," he said excitedly, "and it seems to be coming from the rock. Strike the rock!" he commanded.

The navigator got a mallet and began to hit the rock. At first nothing happened, but then, all of a sudden, the rock split open, and, to everyone's surprise and relief, water started to bubble up out of it in a refreshing fountain.

A great cheer went up as they all rushed forward to drink some cool, fresh water. The family danced for joy, hugging each other and laughing. Now they had plenty of water. They gave the bullock water to drink and filled up all their containers for the rest of the journey.

Relieved and refreshed, the party set off once more after the sun had set. As the moon climbed high into the starlit sky, the navigator guided them safely across the desert, and they finally arrived at the temple after dawn, still in time for their cousin's wedding.

A few hours later, dressed in their finest clothes, they were tucking into a delicious banquet in honour of their beautiful cousin and her new husband. Watching his family enjoy themselves, the father smiled fondly to himself as he silently toasted them with his glass of crystal-clear water. How glad he was that he hadn't given up on them all in the desert.

Life presents all sorts of difficulties and often puts obstacles in our path. On these occasions, it is all too easy to give up. A wise person knows that if they keep trying, they will eventually succeed.

The Lazy
Wood Gatherer

Relax, be very still and listen – listen carefully to this tale about Gabriel, a boy who lived in a small cottage on a cliff overlooking the sea. One day he got into big trouble with his parents. Do you want to know what happened? Let's see if we can find out!

Now ... one sunny day, Gabriel's father, who was a fisherman, asked his son to gather firewood from the forest. They were going on a boat trip the next day to see the whales as a special treat, so they needed wood to light a fire and cook a hearty breakfast before setting off.

But that morning Gabriel was very tired. "It's not fair!" he muttered, "I don't want to gather wood. I just want to take it easy today." Nevertheless, he set off along the path that led to the forest. On his way up the path, he came to a lone tree that had no leaves.

"It's my lucky day!" he exclaimed. "This tree has no leaves and it looks perfect for firewood – dead and dry.

71

I don't need to go all the way to the forest, like father said. I can just rest here and then quickly snap off some branches before I go home." So he sat at the foot of the tree and gazed at the sea spangling in the sunlight. Soon, he fell fast asleep.

Some time later, he awoke with a start – it was getting dark. "Oh no! How long have I been asleep?" he wondered. Jumping up, he climbed the tree and frantically began to break off branches. But, despite appearances, this wood wasn't dead at all – it was green inside and full of sap. And the branches took so much pulling and twisting that one even snapped back and hit him in the eye. Ouch! When he had finally broken off enough branches, he bundled them into his arms, ran back home and piled them outside the house before he went in to bed.

Early next morning, Gabriel's mother rose to prepare breakfast. She picked up the wood to start a fire. But the flames just flickered and died. When her husband came down, she still had no fire. "I'm sorry, breakfast's not ready." she said. "This wood is so green and damp that the fire won't light."

Just then Gabriel appeared. "Son, what's wrong with your eye?" asked his concerned mother.

"And why is this firewood so wet?" growled his father.

The boy gulped and shuffled his feet. He felt ashamed that he had let them down by being so lazy the day before. Trying not to cry, he explained how he had fallen asleep under the tree and gathered the wrong wood, hurting his eye in the process. "I'm so sorry I didn't go to the forest like you asked. I was feeling too tired, so I tried to take an easy way out," he said.

"Well, by the time we gather dry wood to cook breakfast," replied his father, "it'll be much too late to go and see the whales – it's too far."

Gabriel was disappointed, but determined to make amends. Later that day he went to the forest to collect lots of good firewood, so the next morning his mother was able to cook them all a filling breakfast. And as a reward for his hard work, they went to see the whales after all – a magical experience that Gabriel never forgot.

People who are lazy disappoint themselves as well as others. A wise person works hard so that they can enjoy the rewards and have the satisfaction of knowing they did their best.

The Naughty Little Rabbit

Relax, be very still and listen – listen carefully to this tale about a little rabbit who didn't like going to school until, one day, he learned a very important lesson. What do you think it was? Let's see if we can find out!

Now ... in a magical meadow at the foot of a snow-capped mountain lived some lovely furry rabbits. Their leader was so old that his coat had turned silvery grey, and everyone called him Old Silver. He was loved and respected by everyone.

One misty autumn morning as he gazed out of his burrow onto the meadow, he was approached by some eager young rabbits who asked him if he would be kind enough to pass on some of his wisdom. Old Silver twitched his nose. "Why not?" he said. "We'll start tomorrow. Be here at one o'clock sharp and I'll teach you all I know – especially how to avoid being trapped. There's nothing more important than that. Don't be late!"

74

So the next day, at one o'clock on the dot, the rabbits began their classes. All, that is, except one naughty little rabbit called Pip, who didn't think that learning anything could be worth giving up his time playing. He just wanted to have fun. So, day after day, Pip went down to the pond to play with the ducks. He jumped as high as he could to win the attention of passing butterflies. And he went into the woods to hop through the autumn leaves and make tunes from their crunching sounds underfoot.

But one day, when he was busy playing and dancing, he skipped onto a net laid on the ground, which was cunningly covered with twigs and leaves – it was a trap! The net tightened around him, scooping him up into a ball. "Help! I've been caught!" he wailed.

That evening, when Pip didn't return home, his worried mother asked Old Silver to organize a search. He sent the rabbits out to look in the places where Pip usually played, while he himself headed for the places where he knew hunters often laid traps.

He hadn't been searching long when he heard human footsteps. A man was coming – it sounded like a hunter! Alarmed, Old Silver raced on to the next trap and there he found sad little Pip wrapped up in the hunter's net. Quickly, the wise old rabbit used his long, sharp teeth to gnaw through the ropes. Just as the footsteps were almost on top of them, Silver bit through the last strand and Pip was free! They scampered away as fast as their little legs could carry them.

Pip's mother wept with joy when she saw her son unharmed. "I'm so glad you're safe!" she cried. "You gave me such a fright!"

"I'm sorry, mother," said Pip, clinging to her.

"It's all right, son," she replied. "But now do you see why it's so important to create time to listen and learn from others? There are some things in life that you really need to learn."

"Yes, mother, I realize that now," replied Pip. "I'm so sorry, Old Silver! I promise never to skip lessons again."

We can all benefit from listening to the wisdom that others have gained from experience and are kind enough to teach us. A wise person knows that there is a time to play and a time to learn.

The Small
Bowl of Rice

Relax, be very still and listen – listen carefully to this tale about a miser who lived in a big mansion at the top of a lonely hill. One day something happened that was to change his life for ever. Do you want to know what it was? Let's see if we can find out!

Now ... the miser's mansion was very old, big and draughty. He lived there alone, apart from a few servants, and a dog whom he hadn't even bothered to name. The miser slept and ate in one of the mansion's many towers and spent his days counting and recounting his gold. He loved gold more than anything in the world – he never shared or even spent it. And he was renowned for being the meanest man there ever was. He was so mean that he had never invited anyone to his house, nor ever given anyone a present. In fact, he only went out once a year for fear of spending money. And on this day, he would travel in a grand carriage, with his dog and a servant, to collect taxes from the poor peasants who farmed his lands.

One year, he was returning home after a very successful day collecting taxes. Night was falling and, as he hugged his large sack of gold, his carriage was suddenly stopped by robbers. "Help!" he shouted but it was no use. The robbers stripped the miser of his clothes, made him put on rags and took him and his dog far out into the countryside, where they left them with no food or water.

The miser was very shaken up by this turn of events and shouted at the little dog (whom he had never bothered to give a name) for not attacking the robbers. It was getting dark and they were completely lost. Despairing, he crawled under a hedge and cried himself to sleep, thinking of his stolen gold. The little dog curled up in a ball nearby.

The next day, he woke up feeling cold, sore and hungry. He set off with the dog in search of a village, walking and walking, until eventually they came to a road, although they still saw no one. After walking all day without food, the miser felt desperately hungry and sorry for himself. Then, all of a sudden, his dog barked and ran off.

The miser followed him, only to find a lone little cottage surrounded by wild rose bushes. He saw white smoke rising from its chimney. Encouraged, he knocked on the door. But suddenly he hesitated, remembering with shame how he had always sent away anyone who had knocked on his own door for help. Why should anyone want to help a man dressed in rags, such as himself? He was just about to leave when a cheerful voice called, "Who's there?"

Relieved, the miser replied humbly, "I'm sorry to disturb you, but I'm lost and hungry. Could you please spare my dog and I some food? And would there be any chance of letting us sleep somewhere warm?" asked the miser.

"Of course," replied the friendly voice. "Come in."

So the miser went in, and the dog followed. The room was quite bare – there were only a few pieces of old furniture and no curtains on the windows. But there was a small fire in the hearth. Sitting at a table was a kind-looking man, and by his side a brown dog wagged his tail and grinned. The man got up from the table and laughed heartily. "It's a poor lost soul, Archie," he told his dog, "and he's brought you a new friend!"

"Come in and sit down," he said, turning to the miser. "Welcome to my feast. Tonight we have a banquet of delicious rice!" he joked. The man went to a shelf and took down two small bowls. "We'll have to share this rice – it's all I have, I'm afraid," he added. "And your dog can share Archie's." Saying this, he put some rice in Archie's large

81

bowl for the two dogs and divided the rest between the two small bowls for himself and the miser, who couldn't believe the man's generosity. How could he be so poor and yet so happy? The miser thought of his gold, his servants and his mansion. But despite all these possessions, he had never been as happy as this man who had so little. He was filled with guilt and shame for his miserly behaviour over the years.

Soon, his hunger brought him back to the present and he tucked into the rice. He ate it greedily, thinking how nothing had ever tasted so delicious! Soon the miser was infected by the warmth of the kind man's heart and found himself confiding in him about how he had been robbed. The man listened intently, and when the miser had finished, he said, "Your story makes me sad. You have so much yet your life is so lonely and empty." Then, he gave the miser his sleeping spot in front of the fire, said goodnight and lay down on the floor to get a good night's sleep.

The miser was so moved by this kindness, and so grateful for it, that, as he lay awake in front of the fire thinking about what had happened, his mean heart began to melt. Tears streamed down his cheeks, for now he saw how terrible his life really was. He reached out to his dog and patted him for the first time ever. And he resolved to repay the man's generosity a thousand fold.

The next morning, when he awoke, he invited the poor man and his dog to come and live with him in his mansion – an offer which they gladly accepted. Without delay they all set off for the miser's home.

And so it was that from that day forward the miser changed his ways. He and the poor man became the best of friends, living happily together with Archie and Merry – as he named his dog – who flourished with the newfound attention. No one was ever again turned away empty-handed from the mansion on the hill. And instead of collecting taxes, the miser used his gold to improve the lives of local people. Twice a year, he even held feasts for his neighbours and parties for the children, which were so enjoyable that they became the talk of the land.

Greed and selfishness spoil things for everyone. A wise person realizes that the way to true happiness is through sharing whatever they have, no matter how little that may be.

The Prancing Peacock

Relax, be very still and listen – listen carefully to this tale about a handsome but vain peacock. He lived high up in rocky, mountainous country where the white fluffy clouds played in the blue sky over the kingdom of the birds. One afternoon, as the peacock was admiring his reflection in a rock pool, he overheard something very interesting in the chatter of a family of robins. What could it be? Let's see if we can find out!

Now ... on this particular day, Mrs Robin could scarcely contain her excitement. "What a great occasion!" she twittered to her husband as she hopped about.

"Indeed, indeed," agreed Mr Robin.

"Why? What's happening today?" chirped Little Robin with great curiosity.

"Well, my darling," she exclaimed, "today, our king, His Majesty White Swan the Great, is to give the hand of his beautiful daughter, Princess Cygnetta, in marriage."

"Who's she going to marry?" asked Little Robin.

"Well, that's the thing. We don't know yet," said Mr Robin.

"You see," continued Mrs Robin, "many years ago, the king granted Princess Cygnetta a special birthday wish, and she asked to be able to pick her own husband when she was ready to marry. So the king has called all the eligible birds from near and far to meet this evening below the rocky plateau. Today is the day when she will make her choice. Let's hurry – if we arrive early we'll get a good view." So away the three of them flew.

All this time the vain peacock had been listening to the robins' conversation. "Well, well," he muttered to himself, as he turned again to gaze admiringly at his reflection in the rock pool. "Princess Cygnetta is choosing a husband, is she? This might be her lucky day. After all, I'm young, handsome and single – I'm really quite a catch! And it just so happens," he continued to his reflection, "that I'm free this evening. I think I might take a stroll toward the rocky plateau." The peacock turned to go but then stopped to check his appearance one last time. Extremely pleased with his reflection in the pool, he pranced off.

Below the rocky plateau, birds were flying in from all directions, chirping and squawking excitedly as they did so. A large and feathery crowd soon gathered, full of long-legged flamingoes, rainbow-coloured parrots, exotic birds of paradise, wise dignified owls, shimmering humming birds and many more.

Suddenly, King White Swan and Princess Cygnetta appeared on the ledge, and the princess started to look around at the grand gathering of birds. A ripple of excitement went through the crowd as her gaze swept over them, and the young male birds jostled for space to show themselves off. The proud peacock jumped up onto a small rock and opened his beautiful tail feathers, which glistened and shone in the evening light.

Then, the king raised his regal head and opened his great wings. A hush fell over all the birds. "Daughter, my finest subjects stand gathered before us. Are you now ready to choose your husband?" he asked.

The young princess nodded. She had seen the most dazzling bird below and had fallen in love. "That bird over there, father, on that rock. I wish to marry the peacock."

The other young male birds in the crowd sighed with disappointment at first. But they soon cheered the peacock on his good fortune. He puffed out his chest with pride. "Of course," he said smugly, "I knew I'd be chosen! After all, I *am* the most handsome bird of all."

Hearing his boastful words, the other birds began whispering to one another. "What a shame he's so vain. Poor Princess Cygnetta!"

But the peacock was soaking up all the attention and ignored their comments. He fanned out his beautiful tail feathers and bowed to the crowd. Then, he lifted his head up high to show off his strong blue chest. The more everyone admired him, the more he leaned back until – oh dear! – he leaned back so far that he lost his balance and fell clumsily backward. The peacock landed in on his back with a big thump, and an equally loud "Ouchhhh!". How embarassing!

For a moment there was stunned silence, but once the birds saw that he hadn't hurt himself, everyone burst out laughing. What a sorry sight! The peacock's legs were stuck up in the air and his gorgeous tail feathers were all covered in mud. His head spun for a minute, but he quickly pulled himself together, puffing up his chest and fanning out his muddy tail. But when he heard the birds laughing, he shouted, "How *dare* you laugh at me, you commoners! I demand that you show respect to Prince Peacock."

When King White Swan saw the peacock's antics and heard his proud words, he was very angry to see his daughter's chosen husband act so inappropriately.

"Peacock, you are a vain and silly fool," he proclaimed. "Your behaviour today shows that you are not worthy to be my daughter's husband or to become a prince. I will not permit it."

Having been scolded in public, the peacock realized he'd lost his beautiful bride for good and hung his head in shame. And Cygnetta saw she'd had a lucky escape, and asked her father to help her to choose a new husband. While the other birds waited excitedly to see who would be the new choice, the disgraced peacock slunk away, muttering that he'd never be so vain and silly again.

Sometimes it is tempting to show off to others and brag about our special qualities, abilities and achievements. A wise person is confident yet modest about their best traits and talents.

The Dirty Old Goblet

Relax, be very still and listen – listen carefully to this tale about two rival salesmen who wandered from town to town with their carts, trading and selling all sorts of useful and useless things. One man was mean and sly but the other was kind and honest. Do you want to know what happened to them? Let's see if we can find out!

Now ... on this particular day the salesmen were both heading to the same small town to sell their goods. "Morning, Mr Johnson," said kind Mr Wallace politely.

"Where do you think *you're* going?" asked mean Mr Johnson suspiciously.

"I'm going to Little Fulbrook to sell my wares," answered Mr Wallace.

"But, *I'm* selling there," said Mr Johnson. "And I don't want you stealing my business!"

"I understand, and that's fine. Why don't we come to an arrangement to suit us both?" said Mr Wallace.

"Oh all right then," agreed Mr Johnson sulkily, "So while I sell my goods in the north side of town … ".

" … I'll sell mine in the south side so that we're not competing against one another," Mr Wallace chipped in.

"Then, we'll swap over," they both said together.

So it was decided, and the two salesman went off in opposite directions to different parts of town.

Mean Mr Johnson stopped at the first house in the north of the town. He rapped on the door, which was opened by a kindly old lady and a smiling little girl called Ella. Seeing the child, the salesman quickly pulled out several sparkly, plastic bracelets from his pocket and shook them in the light to make them razzle-dazzle. "Would you like to buy a beautiful bracelet for yourself, lovely lady, or perhaps for the sweet little girl?" he said in his best flattering voice.

Ella gasped, "Please grandmother, please can I have the pink one? It's so pretty!"

The old woman stroked the child's hair, saying, "My darling, you know I would buy it for you if I could. But I'm sorry, we need all our money for food." Turning to the man, she said, "Sorry sir, we are poor. We can't afford to buy such luxuries."

"But maybe we could do a swap?" asked Ella. She ran back inside and returned with a dirty, old goblet she had found one day while out playing.

"Please, sir, will you swap the lovely bracelet for this old goblet?" she pleaded.

Mr Johnson picked up the goblet. Noticing it felt heavy, he looked at it closely and scratched the dirt off with his nail. He could see a glint of metal underneath – the goblet was made of gold!

Hiding both his excitement and his greed, he handed it back to the little girl, saying scornfully, "This old goblet is worthless. Nobody would buy it, so I'm afraid you can't have the bracelet."

"Ohhhh ...," sighed Ella sadly, as she ran to her grandmother for a comforting hug.

The mean salesman went on his way, thinking to himself, "I'll return later to say I've changed my mind about the exchange. That way they'll think they've got a great deal! It's so lucky they don't realize what they have – I'll be rich!" And he chuckled to himself, as he thought about how he'd spend all the money that he'd be able to get when he sold the golden goblet.

Meanwhile, kind Mr Wallace had finished selling in the south side of town and now turned to the north. He came to the same house and knocked on the door.

"Good lady and pretty little girl … ," he began cheerily when they answered the door.

"I'm sorry sir," interrupted the lady, "we are poor and can't afford anything. Thank you anyway."

"But grandmother, perhaps *this* kind man will trade something for the goblet?" cried Ella, and she ran off to fetch it again. The old woman whispered to the salesman, "Sir, my granddaughter's goblet is worthless – we were told this only today – so please don't get her hopes up. It would be best if you left before she returns." But the kind salesman felt sorry for her and decided to give her a small gift anyway.

Ella returned and handed him her goblet. Now, this salesman was honest as well as kind. And as soon as he held the goblet and saw the scratch, he exclaimed, "Goodness! What a lucky girl you are! This goblet is solid gold. It's worth more than all the goods on my barrow put together. I'll give you my whole barrow-load and all the money I've earned today in exchange for it."

The old woman and little girl looked at each other in disbelief – they were overjoyed at this fantastic news, and happily agreed to the deal. So kind Mr Wallace gave them all his goods and the day's money in exchange for the goblet. Ella put as many bracelets on her arms as she could wear at once, while her Granny went out to buy delicious food and treats for a celebration dinner.

Later that day, mean Mr Johnson returned to the house. When the old lady answered the door, he cunningly said, "I've changed my mind, I've decided to trade the pink bracelet for that dirty old goblet after all, out of the goodness of my heart."

Ella happily explained that it was too late: they had sold it to a kind salesman and got a lot of money for it as it was real gold! Mr Johnson was furious. He didn't feel any guilt at trying to trick the little girl – he was just angry that he'd missed out on all the money. He abandoned his barrow and ran down the road shouting, "Where are you, Wallace? I saw that goblet first! It's mine!"

But Mr Wallace was long gone. He had already sold the goblet and was sharing out the money to help not only his own family, but also the other families in his village.

When we tell lies, we cause both ourselves and others to suffer, whereas when we tell the truth, we make the world a happier and richer place. A wise person knows that honesty is always the best policy.

The Golden Goose

Relax, be very still and listen – listen carefully to this tale about a little girl called Rosalina, who lived on a rickety old houseboat with her grumpy old aunt. One day, when she was out playing, something amazing happened. What could it be? Let's see if we can find out!

Now ... it had been raining for several days, and little Rosalina was getting really fed up of being cooped up in the house boat. So when the rain finally stopped, she asked her aunt if she could go out to play.

"Yes, but don't go far, as your dinner will be ready soon," said her aunt, as she stirred a big pot on the stove.

So Rosalina put on her shiny red boots and raincoat, and went outside to play. She skipped up and down the river bank, and splished, sploshed and splashed in the muddy puddles.

Then, suddenly she heard a loud honking noise. It seemed to be coming from a clump of tall reeds that grew along the water's edge. But imagine her surprise when she spied a beautiful golden goose there. The bird was flapping his wings and seemed very distressed, as he was tangled up in some old fishing net. When the goose saw her approaching, he became very still and quiet.

"Oh dear, you poor thing. Don't worry, I won't harm you," said Rosalina soothingly. She tiptoed very slowly and cautiously toward the bird so as not to frighten him any more. She stroked his neck and then very gently untangled him from the net. Once free, the goose stretched out his magnificent golden wings and flapped them in gratitude and relief.

"Oh, thank you so much. How can I ever repay you for saving me?" cried the goose, as he danced about in joy. Rosalina laughed and clapped her hands.

"I would like to reward you for what you did. But what can I give you?" he asked.

"You have such beautiful feathers," said Rosalina. "Maybe you could give me one of those?"

"What a good idea!" replied the goose. And he plucked a glistening feather from his golden belly and gave it to the little girl. "If you choose to sell this, you'll get several pieces of gold for it," he continued.

Rosalina held up the feather and it shimmered in the light. "Thank you so much," she said, smiling at the goose. Then, he opened his wings and with a whoosh, flew off.

Rosalina scampered off home. "Auntie! Auntie!" she called as she reached the houseboat. She was hoping that the feather would cheer her aunt up as she had been rather grumpy and unhappy lately.

"What is it, Rosalina? Why are you making so much noise?" her aunt snapped. "And where have you been? Your dinner's getting cold."

Rosalina ran down into the kitchen. With great excitement she told her aunt the whole story about the golden goose. "And look what he gave me as a reward!" she cried, holding up the golden feather.

Rosalina had thought that her aunt would be pleased, but instead she just looked angry. "You silly child!" she scolded. "You only got one feather? Why didn't you ask for more? We could be so rich, we'd never have to worry about money again."

"I'm sorry, Auntie," said Rosalina as she started to cry. "I'll try to find the goose and ask him for more if you want. If I ask him nicely, I think he'll give me another feather."

"Well, go quickly and get as many as you can. Hurry up or the goose will have gone," she said. And as the little girl went on her way, her aunt secretly followed her.

Rosalina ran back up the path until she could see the goose floating serenely on the river. "Dear beautiful golden goose, please come back! I need your help!" she called. And quick as a flash there he was, flying toward her.

But as the goose landed, Rosalina's aunt appeared as if from nowhere and caught him in a net. "Got you!" she exclaimed triumphantly.

"Oh no! What are you doing, Auntie?" cried Rosalina. "Please, don't hurt the goose."

"I'm catching him so that we can take *all* his golden feathers," replied the old woman. She thrust the poor goose under her arm and, ignoring Rosalina's protests, rushed back to the houseboat. There, she took the goose into her kitchen and quickly plucked out all his feathers. By the time Rosalina reached home, the goose was completely bald. And her aunt was smiling at the large pile of golden feathers on the table.

Tears streamed down Rosalina's cheeks as she picked up the goose in her arms. "I'm so sorry," she whispered, gently stroking the bird's neck.

"Rosalina, I want you to look after this goose very well," ordered her aunt. "Then, when its feathers grow back, we can pluck it again. We'll never have to worry about money anymore!" And she rubbed her hands greedily.

So Rosalina tended the goose with love and was very careful to keep him away from her aunt. Slowly he recovered from his terrible experience and, as days turned into weeks, his feathers grew back.

One day Rosalina's aunt decided that it was time to pluck the goose again. She asked her niece to bring her the bird, crowing at the thought of the gold she would soon be spending. But when she saw him, she was furious – his feathers were no longer golden, but a soft downy white.

"Once my golden feathers are all gone, they simply grow back white," he explained. "So, you can't use me any more to get rich." With that, he flew straight out of the window, honking farewell to Rosalina, who felt so happy that he was free, as she watched him disappear among the fluffy clouds floating high in the sky.

When we are greedy, we become unhappy because we never feel that we have enough. A wise person appreciates whatever they have and is thankful for anything they are given.

The Kind and Wise Stag

elax, be very still and listen – listen carefully to this tale about a beautiful stag called Dinos. He lived deep in the heart of a great forest of giant trees with all his animal friends ... until one day everything changed! Do you want to know what happened? Let's see if we can find out!

Now ... Dinos was no ordinary stag – he was the wisest animal in the forest. And he looked special, too, as he had a beautiful amethyst jewel embedded in his forehead and shimmering purple antlers.

When he woke this particular morning, everything was wet, and droplets of rain shone like diamonds on the grass. There had been a big storm during the night, and the dark clouds were just scuttling off over the horizon, as the smiling sun arrived in the sky. As usual, Dinos made his way down to the river for a morning drink. But the storm had made the water angry, so it was surging along faster than usual.

 103

As he stood watching the raging river, he heard a voice calling, "Help! Help! Please help!" Suddenly, a man floated into view, around a bend in the river. He was frantically waving his arms and, every few moments, he disappeared under the water and then bobbed up, spluttering.

The wise stag thought quickly and called out to the man, "Look up! Grab the branches above you!"

The man stretched out his arms, caught hold of a branch and held on tight. Dinos then waded into the water and said to him, "Take hold of my neck."

The man was so shocked to see a stag with shimmering purple antlers and a jewel in his forehead that he let go of the branch. But, thankfully, he just managed to catch hold of Dinos, who pulled him out of the water and up the river bank.

The man, whose name was Arthur, was soaked and exhausted, but immensely grateful to the kind and wise stag. He thanked him time and time again for saving him and asked him what he could do to repay him. "I ask only one thing in return," replied Dinos. "Just give me your word that you will never tell anyone about me or where I live, because there are many wicked and greedy men who will try to hunt me for my jewel."

Full of gratitude, Arthur placed his hand on his heart and vowed never to tell anyone about the stag or where he lived. And then Dinos led the man to a path which would lead him out of the forest.

Several years passed. One day, the queen of the land, who lived far from the great forest, heard a rumour about a wise and beautiful stag with twinkling purple antlers and a magnificent purple jewel in his forehead. Intrigued, she wished to see this splendid animal, and she asked her husband, the king, to find it for her.

Now the king was a kind man who liked to please his wife, so he offered a large reward to anyone who could help him to catch the special stag.

When Arthur heard of the king's search he was overcome by greed and forgot all about the promise he had made to Dinos. He went to the king and led him and his men to the great forest, where they lay in wait for the stag and very soon captured him.

The king was overjoyed to have found the beautiful creature and ordered his men to look after the stag well. They tied him to the back of a cart and gave him fresh hay to eat, and the king even went personally to reassure

  105

the stag that he would not be harmed. But when he saw the stag, he noticed that he was crying. "What's the matter?" he asked gently, "Have my men hurt you?"

A single tear ran down Dinos's cheek. "No, I've been treated very well, thank you. But I'm upset because I think that someone may have betrayed me. I'm very careful to keep away from humans. How did you find me?" he asked softly.

The king was so dismayed to see the stag weeping that he just pointed to greedy Arthur, who had been trying to hide nearby. The man lowered his eyes and looked at the ground. The king asked Dinos, "Do you know this man?"

The stag then told him how he had saved Arthur's life some years before and the man had promised never to tell anyone about him or to mention where he lived.

When the king, who was honest and just, heard that the stag had been captured only because Arthur had broken his promise, he grew red with anger and ordered Arthur to be taken away and taught a lesson.

But the stag, in his compassion, begged the king to forgive the man and let him go. And the king was so moved by the deer's kindness and wisdom that he agreed.

Then, he released the stag and invited him to come and meet his wife the queen, who was so eager to see him after all she had heard about him. Dinos agreed and they all returned to the castle.

The queen and the stag soon became firm friends – she loved to feed him his favourite grapes and he appreciated her gentle kindness. At last the stag felt safe, no longer fearing that he would be hunted for his valuable jewel and antlers. Before long, Dinos became the king's most trusted advisor, helping the monarch to rule the kingdom fairly and wisely by honouring promises made to his subjects and never allowing him to be influenced by greed.

By keeping promises and being kind and forgiving, we make the world a better place for everyone. A wise person shows compassion for others, even when they have been hurt by them.

The Mischievous Monkey

Relax, be very still and listen – listen carefully to this tale about a mischievous monkey who liked to play tricks on an old buffalo. That is, until one day when he learned a very important lesson. Would you like to know what this was? Let's see if we can find out!

Now ... the naughty little monkey and the kind-hearted old buffalo both lived in an ancient forest next to a great grassland. Every day, when the sun was at its highest in the cloudless sky and it got really, really hot, the old buffalo would wander to the edge of the forest and rest in the cool shade of the trees. There, he would doze until the late afternoon. And then, when the heat was not so fierce, he would go out to graze with his herd on the grassland.

As for the mischievous monkey, his home was in the branches of a great tree. And every day, as the other monkeys sat grooming each other and chatting, he liked to wait for the old buffalo to doze off below.

"Hee hee! I think I'll have some fun," he would say gleefully, clapping his little hands.

One day, the monkey waited until he was certain that the buffalo was sound asleep. Then, he swung down and, hanging on to a branch by his tail just above the old buffalo's head, he screeched: "Grooawww!"

The poor buffalo got such a fright. He jumped to his feet and looked around but couldn't see anyone.

"What was that?" he muttered.

"Hee, hee, hee ... got you!" laughed the little monkey, as he threw leaves and nuts down on the old buffalo. Then, he scampered off into the trees, howling with laughter.

The buffalo sighed, shook his head and wandered off. "That little fellow gets naughtier by the day," he thought to himself, and went in search of a quieter place.

Soon he found himself another inviting patch of shade and settled down to finish his afternoon nap. "What a lovely spot!" he said before drifting off to sleep, unaware that he had been followed by his cheeky little "friend".

The monkey had swung over the tree tops and once again sat in the branches, just above the old buffalo, listening carefully. As soon as he heard him start to snore, he crept silently down from the tree and along the ground through the grass to pull the buffalo's tail. "Ow! Ow! Ow!" yelped the startled old buffalo. He got to his feet and was about to leave when he heard laughter.

"Hee, hee, hee ... got you again!" laughed the naughty monkey as he swung up into the tree. Before he disappeared, he looked back and stuck out his tongue at the old buffalo.

"Oh dear ... it looks like I'm not going to get any rest today," lamented the weary old animal.

"You're a big strong buffalo and you have sharp horns, so why do you let that mischievous monkey bother you all the time?" asked a squeaky little voice.

"What? Who said that? Oh, I'm so tired that I must be hearing voices!" said the buffalo to no one in particular.

"Hey, over here!" called the voice.

Looking around again the buffalo spotted the source of the comment – a smiling little snail with a shimmering brown shell, who was sitting on a rock near the tree.

"Oh I'm sorry, Mr Snail, I didn't see you there," said the old buffalo.

"That's all right," chirped Mr Snail, "I'm small and not easy to spot. But you're big and strong. Why don't you put a stop to that little monkey's bad behaviour?"

"I don't like bothering or hurting anyone," replied the buffalo, "not even a tricky little monkey who shows me no respect." The kind-hearted buffalo then bowed to the snail and said, "Thank you for your concern Mr Snail, but please don't worry about me." And he turned to wander back toward the grassland and find his herd.

Later that afternoon, a lone buffalo came to the edge of the forest. He had a very bad temper and because of this all the other buffaloes usually avoided him. He had been walking for many hours and was very tired, so he settled down for a rest at the foot of a tree and fell asleep.

The mischievous monkey was just finishing a rather large banana when he looked down from his branch high up in the tree and noticed the sleeping buffalo.

"Oh, he's back, is he? Time for some more mischief!" the monkey chuckled to himself, not noticing that this was a different buffalo.

So, he swung down from branch to branch and somersaulted through the air onto the sleeping buffalo's back. The lone buffalo roared and shot to his feet. "What

do you think you're doing?" he growled, as he threw the little monkey off his back with all his might.

"Ouch!" cried the monkey, as he hit the ground with a thud. Shocked, he realized that it was the wrong buffalo. And now he was in big trouble because the angry buffalo was about to charge at him. The monkey froze with fear.

Suddenly, from out of nowhere, the kind old buffalo appeared, warded off the furious beast and gently scooped the little monkey to safety! The wild buffalo stamped his foot, snorted and trotted off unhappily.

"Oh, thank you!" cried the little monkey gratefully to the old buffalo, "But I've been so mean to you. Why did you take the trouble to save me?"

"It was nothing," replied the wise old buffalo modestly, "I just try to treat everyone as I'd like to be treated myself." And with that, he trundled off to have a rest in another lovely patch of shade he'd spotted.

Often we don't give enough thought to our behaviour. A wise person acts with respect and sympathy toward all beings, treating them in the same way that they'd like to be treated themselves.

The Whatnot Fruit

Relax, be very still and listen – listen carefully to this tale about some travellers who arrived one evening at the edge of a village. They were tired, so they decided to stop for the night and were looking forward to a well-earned rest. That is, until they discovered an exotic fruit and suddenly everything changed. Do you want to know what happened? Let's see if we can find out!

Now ... setting up camp was a busy time for the travellers. They bustled around as they lifted colourful carpets from their caravans and laid them out on the ground. Then, they gathered wood and built a big fire. Soon, pots and pans were rattling away merrily on the fire, sending delicious aromas floating over the little camp. And when dinner was finally ready, everyone gathered together around the fire to eat.

After they had eaten all their food, a little girl called Polly, one of the children of the group, turned to her mother and pointed to a huge tree full of sweet and juicy-looking, orange-coloured fruits. "Mother," she said, "I'm still a little hungry. Please may we have some fruits from that tree for dessert? They look so delicious!" Her mother looked at the tree and frowned.

"Yes, they do look tempting. But I don't recognize that tree or its fruits. You know that we shouldn't eat anything we don't recognize or haven't eaten before – they could turn out to be poisonous."

"But they look like big juicy mangoes!" said Polly.

"Well, the fruits do *look* like mangoes, but the tree doesn't look like a mango *tree*," replied her mother. "So I'm not sure. See what your father thinks."

"Father, father, can we eat some fruits from that tree? Pleeease!" pleaded Polly. Together, Polly and her father went over to the tree and he picked one of the brightly-coloured fruits. He sniffed it and then let it drop to the ground.

"Listen, Polly, listen children," he said. "I know you're all tempted to eat these orange fruits, but I don't think that they're mangoes, so we shouldn't take a chance. As your mother said, we don't know what fruits they really are, so none of us should eat them."

116

But Polly wasn't listening and she picked up the fruit that her father had dropped. Her mouth was watering because it looked so delicious. She turned her back to the others. "What harm could it do if I just have one little bite?" she thought to herself.

Before anyone could notice she had peeled back a patch of the fruit's skin and bitten into the juicy flesh. "Mmm, it's so sweet!" she exclaimed, and took another bite. Some of the other children saw her and copied her.

"Polly!" cried her mother. " What are you doing?"

Polly turned to face her mother, the juice from the fruit staining her lips. "I … I feel a little strange … ," she started to say, but the look of disbelief on her mother's face stopped her mid-sentence.

"You're turning orange like the fruit!" her mother cried.

Polly looked down at her fingers, which were gradually going bright orange, and watched, spellbound, as the carroty colour spread down her legs. She was now orange from the top of her head to the tip of her toes!

There were shrieks of disbelief as the other few children who had eaten the fruit started to turn orange, too. No one knew what to do, as, one by one, the orange children fell deeply sleep. Their parents tried to wake them up, but with no success. Some of the travellers went to the small huts of the local village to ask for help, but no one answered their door. So the worried parents kept watch over their children all night.

Even when the birds started to sing their dawn chorus, and the sun climbed above the nearby hill, Polly and her friends still lay fast sleep – and bright orange.

Now, in the past when travellers had come to this village, nearly *all* of them had eaten fruit from the tempting tree – which the villagers called the "Whatnot" fruit. Then, while the travellers were sleeping, the bad villagers would creep out and help themselves to all their possessions. And so it was this morning that the village thieves came to steal, as usual. But this time, when they got to the camp, they were surprised to find everyone, except a few children, awake. When the travellers saw the villagers, they asked them for help, but the thieves were so shocked that they could only ask, "How come you didn't *all* eat the Whatnot fruits? Everyone else always has."

"Well, firstly, we didn't recognize the fruits so we didn't think they were safe," replied Polly's father. "And secondly, we wondered why so much ripe fruit was left unpicked on a tree next to a village – it seemed very strange."

"You're very wise, and your caution has saved you," confessed one of the thieves. "Usually, once the travellers have eaten the fruit and fallen asleep, we take their things. I know it's wrong, but we're very poor," he said, ashamed.

"Well," said Polly's father, "How about making a deal? *We* won't tell anyone about this if *you* explain to us how to waken our children, as well as pick all the Whatnot fruits, bury them and promise never to trick people in this way again. We'll be back to check."

The thieves didn't want their village to get a bad name, so they agreed. "The fruit is harmless," they said reassuringly. "Your children are just in an enchanted sleep. They'll wake up in a few hours and feel completely normal." And, indeed, it wasn't long before the sleeping children began to stir, and to everyone's relief, they soon returned to their normal colour and their usual selves.

Polly learned from this experience and always tried to listen to others' advice and to resist temptation. But she never forgot the tantalizing taste of the Whatnot fruit. Sometimes she longed to take a big juicy bite again ... and one day she did just that – but only in a dream!

If something appears too good to be true –
it probably is. A wise person knows that no
matter how tempting something appears, it
is always prudent to act with caution.

The Lion and the Jackal

Relax, be very still and listen – listen carefully to this tale about a mighty lion who lived on a vast, grassy plain. Although he was a kind lion, most of the animals feared him, and he didn't have many friends. But all that was to change when, one day, the lion found himself in trouble. Do you want to know what happened? Let's see if we can find out!

Now … on this particular day, the lion set off to explore the far side of the plain. After some time, he began to feel thirsty, so he went down to the great lake to get a drink. He waded a little way in and lapped up the cool, fresh water. But as he tried to return to the water's edge, he felt himself slowly sinking into the mud.

He tried to pull himself free, but the more he struggled the more he stuck fast. He looked to the sun for help, but the sun was taking a rest from shining, behind some thick dark clouds. The lion was still stuck

121

when nighttime came, and the moon climbed into the dark sky. He called to the moon for help, but she was too busy chatting to a star to hear him. Soon he began to give up hope of ever being rescued.

Just then a little jackal came along, singing to himself. "Goodness me! A lion!" he exclaimed. Terrified, the startled jackal was about to jump for cover into the undergrowth when the lion called out to him.

"Help me! Please, Mr Jackal, help me – I'm completely stuck in this mud."

"The king of the jungle wants help from me?" thought the jackal in amazement. Turning to the lion he said, "But if I free you, you'll just gobble me up!"

"I won't, I promise. I'm a lion of my word. Please don't be afraid," said the lion. "If you help to free me, I'll be your friend for ever."

The jackal was a kind soul who didn't like to see anyone suffer, so he gathered all his courage and approached the lion. With a lot of huffing and puffing and scrabbling around, he dug the mud from around the lion's great paws. The lion tried really hard to pull his paws free and, one by one, managed to lift them out of the mud. Then he scrambled up the bank, shook his great mane, threw back his head and roared, "I'm free! And it's all thanks to you, my friend. It's late and dark, and I live far from here. Would you help me again by letting me stay at your home tonight?" he asked.

"Well … er … ," started the jackal reluctantly.

"Of course, I give you my word that I won't harm you or your family," interrupted the lion, who could see that his new friend was worried.

"Well, if you promise … I suppose … Yes, you're welcome to come, but my home is small and plain," replied the jackal, who decided that he could trust the lion.

Off they went to the jackal's home. Mrs Jackal was very startled to see the lion, and the little jackal pups were so frightened that they ran to hide behind her back.

"Don't worry, my dears. The lion is my friend," said the jackal proudly, and he explained how he had rescued him from the mud. Mrs Jackal was still rather suspicious.

But then the lion said, "Today you did me a great service, my friend. As the king of the jungle, I would like to repay you for all your kindness by taking care of you and your family from now on. I would like you to come and live with me and my family in our luxurious royal den."

After some discussion, the jackals agreed, and so the next morning they all set off to the lion's den. The families lived happily together and, as time went by, the lion and the jackal became the best of friends.

However, the lioness gradually began to resent their friendship, fearing that the lion loved the jackal family more than his own family. It started as a small thought, but the more she dwelled upon it, the more the seed of jealousy grew in her heart until it had taken over all her thoughts. One day, she decided that they had to go.

From then on, whenever she was alone with Mrs Jackal, the lioness would find fault with her or criticize the little jackal pups.

At first, Mrs Jackal ignored the lioness's unkind ways, but eventually, after a particularly horrible day, Mrs Jackal said to her husband, "I fear we are no longer welcome here. Mrs Lion complains about everything I do. The lion must want us to leave."

Now, the jackal didn't believe that the lion would break his promise, so he went straight to him and said, "My friend, perhaps we have outstayed our welcome in your home – your wife no longer seems to want us here. Would you like us to leave?"

Surprised, the lion asked his wife, "My dear, is this true? Do you want our friends to go?"

Mrs Lion looked up sadly and replied, "I'm sorry, but these days you seem to put the jackal family before your own. You don't appear to care much about us any more."

"My darling wife!" replied the lion. "Let me assure you that my love for you and our cubs is in no way lessened by my love for our friends. When the jackal saved my life, I became forever in his debt, so I offered him and his family my protection. Caring for them only enriches my love for you and our cubs."

Hearing this, the lioness felt very ashamed of her jealousy. She apologized again and again to the jackal family and after that day she became firm friends with the lovely Mrs Jackal.

From then on, the two families spent the rest of their days enjoying each other's company, without further resentment or arguments. And their descendants lived happily together for generations to come.

Sometimes it is easy to let fear and jealousy cloud our judgment. A wise person knows that there is enough love in their heart to give to every living creature in the world.

The Prince with a Lot to Learn

Relax, be very still and listen – listen carefully to this tale about a young prince, who lived in a lavish palace in the desert. He loved to play all day with his friends. That is, until one day a stranger appeared and everything changed. Do you want to know what happened? Let's see if we can find out!

Now … the prince and his friends were happily playing ball in the courtyard when they heard a knock on the big wooden door. They stopped their games in surprise, for the palace was so remote that there were seldom visitors. "Let's go and see who it is!" shouted the young prince. A servant opened the door and there stood a tall, bearded, simply-dressed man looking down at him with a twinkle in his eye.

"Good morning, sir," said the prince, as he greeted the stranger. "Have you come to see my father, the king?"

"Good morning, Your Highness," replied the stranger. "No, I'm actually here to see you. I'm going to be your

teacher." The young prince's smile faded. "I see …, " he replied gravely.

His parents had told him that some day he would have to learn all the things a king should know. He was just surprised that the time had come so soon. The young prince bowed to the man, who bowed in return, and then his new teacher followed the servant to be presented to the king.

That night, when the queen was tucking the prince into bed, she noticed he was unusually quiet. She looked into his eyes and said, "My dear son. You're growing into a man. When your father and I become too old to rule, our great nation will be in your hands."

"But I don't want to grow up," he replied.

"I know," she said, as she smiled and kissed him goodnight, "but everything will be just fine."

From then on the prince spent his days learning about his country and the world beyond. He was introduced to important people and observed his father at work. In short, he was taught everything that made a man worthy to be a king.

Years passed, and the prince grew tall, strong and wise. Then one morning, the teacher calmly closed his book and said, "Your Highness,

I have taught you all I know and my work here is done. It's time for me to leave."

The prince had always known that this day would come, yet he loved and respected his teacher so much that he begged him to stay. But the teacher gently said it was time to move on.

The prince wept as his teacher departed. The queen wiped away his tears, saying, "Be at peace. Everything has its time, and nothing lasts forever. Your days of study are over, and soon you will be King."

Before long the prince was indeed King. He married a princess from a distant land and they had a beautiful daughter. One day, when the little princess was playing with her friends, there was a knock on the castle door. "Let's go and see who it is!" she shouted. The door opened and standing there was a tall, bearded, simply-dressed man looking down at her with a twinkle in his eye …

It is only natural to want things to stay as they are, but life is a journey and change is unavoidable. A wise person accepts this and enjoys each precious moment as fully as they can.

Goblin
Island

Relax, be very still and listen – listen carefully to this tale about a crew of adventurous sailors who got caught in a ferocious storm. Do you want to know what happened? Let's see if we can find out!

Now … one day, as the sailors' ship was bobbing up and down in the breeze, a great black storm cloud sprang out of the blue sky and whipped the sea into a frothing rage. Their boat was rocked to and fro for hours, until it crashed into some rocks. There it lay until the storm finally passed, and when the dazed sailors looked around them, they found themselves on a beautiful beach of glistening sand fringed with lush palm trees. They couldn't believe their luck – it looked like paradise! Then, out of nowhere, appeared a group of beautiful women, carrying baskets of delicious fruits and new clothes, and inviting them to stay in their huts. And so it was that, for days on end, the sailors were treated like kings by these women, being fed one scrumptious meal after another. It all seemed too good to be true – so much so that they forgot all about their normal lives and their families and friends waiting at home.

After several days, a sailor asked one of the women why there were no men on the island. She replied that they had sailed away many years ago and never returned. That night the same sailor heard voices, so he crept from his bed to the next hut and listened at the door. "We need to fatten them up and eat them before they escape," said a woman's voice.

Peeping through a crack in the door, the sailor saw – to his astonishment – a group of ugly goblins instead of the beautiful women he had expected! "We've been tricked!" he gasped. "They're not women, but goblins in disguise, and they're feeding us up so we're juicy to eat!"

In the morning, he told his fellow sailors what he'd seen and heard. When they realized they'd been deceived, they were all terribly frightened – all, that is, except for one big strong sailor, "You must have been dreaming!" he insisted, "These beautiful women can't possibly be goblins. I'm not leaving."

While he stomped off back to the huts, the others fell to their knees and begged the gods of the happy lands to help them. One of the gods, who had been watching all along, was pleased they had realized their mistake and decided to help them. In a flash, he changed himself into a magnificent winged silver horse, and flew to the island. The grateful sailors climbed onto his back, sadly leaving behind their stubborn shipmate who still didn't believe the truth. However, just as the great horse began to spread his wings, they were overjoyed to see the last sailor come sprinting after them and clamber gratefully onto the horse's back. "I saw goblins heating the pot to cook us in!" he spluttered. "I'm sorry I wouldn't listen – I just didn't want to believe it." And his last words were whisked away by the wind as the horse flew effortlessly up and up into the sky to safety, until Goblin Island was just a tiny speck in the great blue ocean.

It can be tempting to ignore the facts when we wish that they were different. A wise person knows the importance of facing up to the truth and they tackle every challenge head on.

Learning to Meditate

Although the practice of meditation is often associated with Eastern philosophy and religion, we are all born with the innate ability to meditate, so it can be done by anyone of any age or creed. Even if we don't know it, we have all, at times, experienced its calming effects when we were completely absorbed in a particular activity – for example, while listening to music, watching a sunset or engaged in a particular hobby. At such times, we feel contented, peaceful and at one with the world. By learning to consciously meditate, we can bring this same deep focus into our everyday life, so that it gradually becomes our abiding state of being, rather than a occasional, brief experience.

It can be useful to explain the concept of meditation to your child as going on a journey of adventure or discovery. This will encourage them to be open to and to learn to work with whatever unfolds. However, it's important to make sure that they feel safe and that they know they can stop at any time if they become uncomfortable or tired.

It's good to set aside 5 to 10 minutes each day in which to do a guided meditation (see pages 136–9) with your child. You may like to incorporate this into their bedtime routine – either instead of or after reading one of the stories in this book, which, of course, have a powerful meditative quality themselves in that they focus your child's attention and encourage them to visualize settings, characters and events.

Encourage older children, who may be ready to meditate on their own, to start with 5 minutes per day, and gradually build up to 10 or 15 minutes. Naturally, the length of time that they are able to sit for will vary from child to child, but they will soon get an idea of what is appropriate by how it makes them feel. The quality of the meditation session is more important than its length, and the more regularly they practice, the greater the benefits they will enjoy. Try to get your child to meditate at the same time in the same place each day. In the evening, just before going to bed, is the best time for most people, as they can go to sleep straight afterward. However, they should feel free to practise in the morning or at any other time of the day, if they prefer.

It's a good idea to be fully prepared before meditation. Your child should wear warm, loose clothing and should wash their hands and face before beginning to cleanse themselves symbolically of their everyday activities. Then choose a quiet place where interruptions are unlikely, turn off any phones and dim any lights. When all the practical preparations have been completed, they can relax and get comfortable by doing the pre-meditation relaxation exercise on pages 24–5.

In order to get the most from meditation, it's important that your child learns how to sit well. They need to be comfortable and relaxed yet fully alert while they practise, so it's best if they sit either on a cushion on the floor or on a bed, with their back straight but unsupported. They should close their eyes and rest their hands loosely in their lap.

If you are guiding your child's meditation, speak in a very slow, relaxed voice, pausing from time to time to let your words sink in, so that they can follow you easily and/or conjure up the scene as vividly as possible. It's also important to let them know that it's quite natural for their mind to get distracted or to wander, and that if this happens, all they have to do is bring their attention back to their body.

Metta Meditation

This meditation is derived from the traditional Buddhist practice called *metta bhavana*, which is a Pali term meaning "the development of loving-kindness". The word *bhavana* means to develop or cultivate; while *metta* means "love" – not in a romantic sense but instead a heartfelt warmth or kindness for yourself and all other living beings.

By meditating on loving-kindness, you can enhance not only positive feelings toward yourself but also toward family, friends, acquaintances and, ultimately, all beings, making compassionate behaviour an integral part of everyday life. Metta is particularly useful for transforming negative feelings into positive ones. Your child can tap into it any time they are feeling jealous, angry or upset – for example, after they have had an argument with a friend. More broadly, the meditation opposite will help them to become less selfish and more tolerant, which will, in turn, encourage more positive emotions and responses from all those with whom they come into contact.

Begin the meditation by inviting your child to sit comfortably with their eyes closed. Ask them to breathe deeply for a moment or two. Then, gently read the exercise out loud to them. You might like to join in the meditation on loving-kindness yourself.

"So with a boundless heart
Should one cherish all living beings:
Radiating kindness over the entire world."
THE BUDDHA

"Focus your attention on your body and smile as broadly as you can. Feel your heart get bigger as you smile. Imagine yourself surrounded by beautiful golden light and say: 'May I be happy – may I be really happy from my head right down to my toes.' Then say: 'I love myself dearly.'

Now imagine all your family – your mother and father, brothers and sisters, grandparents, uncles, aunts, cousins and pets. In your mind's eye see them standing in front of you, smiling, surrounded by beautiful golden light, and say: 'May my family be happy – may they be really happy from their heads right down to their toes.' Then, say: 'I love my family dearly.'

Now think of your friends, teachers and neighbours. Imagine them standing in front of you, smiling, surrounded by beautiful golden light, and say: 'May my friends, teachers and neighbours be happy – may they be really happy from their heads right down to their toes.' Then, say: 'I love my friends, teachers and neighbours dearly.'

Next, bring your focus back to yourself and see the golden light that surrounds you spreading out to all the people and animals in the world. Imagine the Earth surrounded by a beautiful golden light and say: 'May all beings be happy – may they be really happy from their heads right down to their toes.' Then, say: 'I love all beings and accept love from all of them, too.'

Now slowly wiggle your toes and fingers, and open your eyes. Try to keep this love for everyone in your heart at all times."

Rainbow Meditation

Rainbows lift our mood with their bright colours when they appear, as if by magic, after rain. This meditation encourages your child to draw positive inspiration from the colours of a rainbow to boost their self-confidence. Ask them to sit comfortably with their eyes closed.

"Take a deep breath in ... and out, and feel your body relax. Picture yourself surrounded by red light. Imagine breathing in the red light, and it filling you with energy.

Now see yourself surrounded by orange light. Imagine breathing in the orange light, and it filling you with strength.

Next, visualize yourself surrounded by yellow light. Imagine breathing in the yellow light, and it filling you with happiness.

Then, picture yourself surrounded by green light. Imagine breathing in the green light, and it filling you with friendship.

Now see yourself surrounded by blue light. Imagine breathing in the blue light, and it filling you with peace.

Next, picture yourself surrounded by indigo light. Imagine breathing in the indigo light, and it filling you with gentleness.

Now, visualize yourself surrounded by violet light. Imagine breathing in the violet light, and it filling you with love.

Finally, imagine a bright rainbow carrying all this energy, strength, happiness, friendship, peace, gentleness and love from your heart into your home, your street, your town, your country ... the whole world. Slowly let the rainbow fade. Breathe slowly as you relax. Now wiggle your toes and fingers, and open your eyes."

Breathing Meditation

By focusing on deep, rhythmical breathing, this meditation not only helps your child to develop concentration and tame the natural tendency for their mind to wander, it also teaches them to hold their attention in each and every moment. Ask them to sit comfortably with their eyes closed and their hands resting on their tummy.

"Take a deep breath in ... and out. Breathe in slowly and feel your tummy get bigger. Breathe out slowly and feel your body relax. Again breathe in slowly and feel your tummy get bigger, and breathe out slowly and feel your body relax. Now imagine that you are standing on a beautiful beach. There are palm trees swaying and the beach has glittering golden sand. There are sandcastles dotted around, each of which has its own little flag, fluttering in the breeze. It's warm and sunny, and there's a clear blue sky. What a lovely day! Stand at the edge of the sea for a few moments and feel the cool water gently lap your toes, as the waves come in and go out, come in and go out ... Allow this gentle rhythm to guide your breathing – breathe in each time the waves come into the shore and breathe out each time they go back out to sea. Allow your breath to follow the inward and outward rhythm of the waves over and over again. Each time you breathe in, feel your tummy get bigger, and each time you breathe out, feel your body relax. Now let the beach fade away in your mind and just sit, breathing gently, for a moment. When you are ready, wiggle your toes and fingers, and open your eyes."

139

Index of Values and Issues

These two complementary indexes cover the specific topics that the 20 stories of this book are designed to address directly or by implication. The same topics are covered from two different perspectives: positive (Values) and negative (Issues). Each index reference consists of an abbreviated story title, followed by the page number on which the story begins.

VALUES

A

acceptance,
of blame, Bull, 43, Wood Gatherer, 71
of change, Sticky Hair, 37, Rice, 79, Prince, 127
of growing up, Prince, 127
of learning new things, Sticky Hair, 37, Kingshuk, 59, Rabbit, 74, Prince, 127
of life's changes, Lion, 121, Prince, 127
of mistakes, Bull, 43, Wood Gatherer, 71, Rabbit, 74, Rice, 74, Peacock, 84, Whatnot Fruit, 115, Goblin, 131
of others, Rice, 79, Lion, 121,
of others' appearance, Elephant, 48, Rice, 79
of others' behaviour, Monkey, 108, Goblin, 131
of others' knowledge, Sticky Hair, 37, Quails, 55, Kingshuk, 59, Prince, 127
of own appearance, Sticky Hair, 37
of own stupidity, Peacock, 84
of responsibility, Desert, 65
of situation, Desert, 65, Monkey, 108
of time passing, Prince, 127
of the truth, Goblin, 131
of unknown creatures, plants and places, Sticky Hair, 37, Kingshuk, 59
of wrongdoing, Bull, 43, Wood Gatherer, 71, Rice, 79, Whatnot Fruit, 115

achievement,
sense of, Parrot, 27, Quails, 55, Desert, 65

affection,
for friends and loved ones, Parrot, 27, Bull, 43, Elephant, 48, Goose, 97, Stag, 103, Lion, 121, Prince, 127

ambitions,
realizing, Prince, 127

appreciation,
of adventure, Goblin, 131
of animals and birds, Goose, 97, Stag, 103
of beautiful things, Kingshuk, 59, Goose, 97, Stag, 103
of discoveries, Kingshuk, 59, Desert, 65, Goblet, 90
of environment, Desert, 59, Goblin, 131
of intelligence, Sticky Hair, 37, Desert, 65, Rabbit, 74, Prince, 127
of kindness, Goose, 97, Stag, 103, Monkey, 108, Lion, 121
of laughter, Elephant, 48
of learning from others, Kingshuk, 59, Desert, 65, Rice, 79, Prince, 127
of nature, Kingshuk, 59
of others, Sticky Hair, 37, Bull, 43, Elephant, 48, Goose, 97, Stag, 103, Monkey, 108, Lion, 121, Prince, 127
of the moment, Elephant, 48, Kingshuk, 59, Rice, 79
of what you have, Bull, 43, Elephant, 48, Goblet, 90, Goose, 97
of wisdom, Stag, 103, Prince, 127

awareness,
of animal life, Goose, 97, Stag, 103
of beauty of nature, Kingshuk, 59, Goose, 97, Stag, 103, Goblin, 131
of change, Turtle, 33, Peacock, 84, Prince, 127, Goblin, 131
of danger, Parrot, 27, Quails, 55, Desert, 65, Rabbit, 74, Monkey, 108, Goblin, 131, Whatnot Fruit, 115, Lion, 121, Goblin, 131
of environment, Desert, 65, Rabbit, 74, Whatnot Fruit, 115, Goblin, 131
of others, Elephant, 48, Rice, 79, Goose, 97, Lion, 121

of others' feelings, Bull, 43, Elephant, 48, Rice, 79
of own feelings, Sticky Hair, 37, Rice, 79
of own good fortune, Elephant, 48, Rice, 79, Goblet, 90
of own intelligence, Sticky Hair, 37, Rabbit, 74, Prince, 127
of seasons, Kingshuk, 59
of time passing, Turtle, 33, Desert, 65, Prince, 127
of weather, Turtle, 33, Desert, 65
of what's around you, Parrot, 27, Turtle, 33, Quails, 55, Rice, 79, Goblin, 131

B

belief,
in others, Sticky Hair, 37, Bull, 43, Quails, 55, Stag, 103
in own actions, Parrot, 27, Desert, 65
in self, Parrot, 27, Sticky Hair, 37, Desert, 65

belonging,
sense of, Elephant, 48, Rice, 79, Stag, 107, Lion, 121

bravery,
in face of danger, Parrot, 27, Sticky Hair, 37, Rabbit, 74, Lion, 121
in facing new situations, Prince, 127

C

calmness,
in scary situations, Parrot, 27, Sticky Hair, 37, Desert, 65, Rabbit, 74

caring,
for nature, Kingshuk, 59
for others, Parrot, 27, Sticky Hair, 37, Bull, 43, Elephant, 48, Rabbit, 74, Rice, 79, Goblet, 90, Goose, 97, Stag, 103, Monkey, 108, Lion, 121

caution,
acting with, Whatnot Fruit, 115, Goblin, 131

challenges,
accepting, Parrot, 27, Sticky Hair, 37, Bull, 43, Prince, 127, Goblin, 131

change,
accepting, Prince, 127
in life's path, Rice, 79, Lion, 121, Prince, 127
in seasons, Turtle, 33, Kingshuk, 59
of attitude, Sticky Hair, 37, Bull, 43, Elephant, 48, Wood Gatherer, 71, Rice, 79, Peacock, 84, Whatnot Fruit, 115

choices,
making good, Turtle, 33, Quails, 55, Desert, 65, Rabbit, 74, Rice, 79, Peacock, 84, Lion, 121, Goblin, 131

communicating,
with others, Bull, 43, Elephant, 48, Kingshuk, 59, Rabbit, 74, Rice, 79, Goblin, 131

compassion, Parrot, 27, Bull, 43, Elephant, 48, Rice, 79, Goose, 97, Stag, 103, Monkey, 108, Lion, 121

concentration, Parrot, 27, Bull, 43

confidence,
in group situations, Quails, 55, Goblin, 131
inner, Desert, 65, Lion, 121

co-operating,
with others, Quails, 55, Whatnot Fruit, 115, Lion, 121, Goblin, 131

consideration,
for others, Parrot, 27, Turtle, 33, Elephant, 48, Rice, 79, Goblet, 90, Goose, 97, Stag, 103, Lion, 121

contentment,
finding, Elephant, 48, Rice, 79, Stag, 103, Lion, 121

courage,
  in face of danger, Parrot, 27, Sticky Hair, 37, Desert, 65, Rabbit, 74, Lion, 121, Goblin, 131
  of own convictions, Parrot, 27, Sticky Hair, 37, Bull, 43, Lion, 121, Goblin, 131
  when doing difficult tasks, Parrot, 27, Lion, 121
  when making choices, Goblin, 131
curiosity,
  in others, Elephant, 48, Kingshuk, 59

D
dana (giving freely – see p.13), Parrot, 27, Elephant, 48, Rabbit, 74, Rice, 79, Lion, 121
decisions,
  making brave, Parrot, 27, Lion, 121
  making wise, Sticky Hair, 37, Elephant, 48, Quails, 55, Desert, 65, Whatnot Fruit, 115, Lion, 121
determination,
  to achieve ambitions, Kingshuk, 59
  to make amends, Wood Gatherer, 71, Rice, 79
  to succeed, Parrot, 27, Sticky Hair, 37, Bull, 43, Quails, 55, Desert, 65
dhyana (concentration – see p.13), Parrot, 27, Desert, 65, Prince, 127
discipline,
  self-, Whatnot Fruit, 115, Prince, 127

E
effort,
  to do hard work, Desert, 65, Prince, 127
  to do something difficult, Parrot, 27, Bull, 43
  to get along with others, Quails, 55
emotions,
  changing, Rice, 79, Goblin, 131
  showing, Bull, 43, Elephant, 48
encouragement,
  of others, Bull, 43, Desert, 65, Goblin, 131
enjoyment, (see also pleasure)
  of beauty, Kingshuk, 59, Goose, 97, Stag, 103
  of comfort and safety, Elephant, 48, Rice, 79, Stag, 103
  of discoveries, Kingshuk, 59, Goblet, 90

of entertainment, Rice, 79
of environment, Rabbit, 74
of friends, Elephant, 48, Rice, 79, Stag, 103, Lion, 121
of nature, Kingshuk, 59
of others, Sticky Hair, 37, Elephant, 48, Rice, 79, Stag, 103
of parties, Rice, 79
of quiet times alone, Monkey, 108
of the moment, Kingshuk, 59, Rice, 79, Prince, 127
ethical behaviour, (see sila), Elephant, 48, Goblet, 90, Stag, 103, Lion, 121
excitement,
  of learning, Kingshuk, 59, Rabbit, 74, Prince, 127
  of success, Desert, 65
exploring,
  feelings, Rice, 79
  life's options, Rice, 79, Goblin, 131
  new places, Lion, 121

F
fairness, Stag, 103, Lion, 121
faith,
  in others, Turtle, 33, Bull, 43, Quails, 55, Kingshuk, 59, Rabbit, 74, Lion, 121, Goblin, 131
  in self, Parrot, 27, Sticky Hair, 37, Desert, 65, Stag, 103
feelings,
  exploring, Elephant, 48
  understanding others', Sticky Hair, 37, Bull, 43, Elephant, 48, Rice, 79, Lion, 121
forgiveness, Bull, 43, Stag, 103, Monkey, 108
friends,
  benefiting from, Parrot, 27, Elephant, 48, Rice, 79, Lion, 121, Goblin, 131
  making, Sticky Hair, 37, Elephant, 48, Rice, 79

G
generosity, (see also sharing)
  of praise, Bull, 43
  of spirit, Parrot, 27, Rice, 79, Peacock, 84, Monkey, 108
  toward others, Elephant, 48, Rice, 79, Goblet, 90, Lion, 121

gentleness,
  toward others, Sticky Hair, 37, Elephant, 48, Goose, 97, Stag, 103, Monkey, 108
giving,
  to others, Elephant, 48, Rabbit, 74, Rice, 79, Goose, 97
  your best, Parrot, 27, Desert, 65
gratitude,
  for what you have, Elephant, 48, Rice, 79, Goblet, 90
  for what you have seen, Kingshuk, 59
  toward others, Parrot, 27, Sticky Hair, 37, Bull, 43, Elephant, 48, Rice, 79, Goose, 97, Stag, 103, Monkey, 108, Lion, 121, Prince, 127, Goblin, 131

H
happiness,
  dancing for joy, Desert, 65, Goose, 97
  inner, Rice, 79
  in others' company, Sticky Hair, 37, Elephant, 48, Rice, 79
  in succeeding, Parrot, 27, Bull, 43, Desert, 65
  knowing people love you, Sticky Hair, 37, Elephant, 48
  laughing with joy, Elephant, 48, Desert, 65
  making others happy, Rice, 79, Goose, 97
  sense of, Kingshuk, 59, Goblet, 90
  sharing with others, Elephant, 48, Kingshuk, 59, Rice, 79, Goose, 97
harmony,
  living in, Elephant, 48, Sticky Hair, 37, Rice, 79, Stag, 103, Lion 121
help,
  accepting, from others, Turtle, 33, Rice, 79, Goose, 97, Lion, 121, Goblin, 131
helping others, Parrot, 27, Turtle, 33, Elephant, 48, Desert, 65, Rabbit, 74, Rice, 79, Goose, 97, Stag, 103, Monkey, 108, Lion, 121
  when things get difficult, Parrot, 27, Goblin, 131
  with things you've never done before, Rice, 79
honesty, Goblet, 90, Stag, 103
humility, Peacock, 84, Whatnot, 115

I
imagination,
  power of, Kingshuk, 59, Desert, 65
impermanence,
  accepting, Prince, 127
independence,
  gaining, Prince, 127
ingenuity, Parrot, 27, Turtle, 33, Sticky Hair, 37, Quails, 55, Desert, 65
initiative,
  taking, Parrot, 27, Turtle, 33, Sticky Hair, 37, Quails, 55, Desert, 65, Stag, 103, Goblin, 131
insights,
  learning from other people's, Kingshuk, 59, Prince, 127
inspiration,
  finding, Sticky Hair, 37
  gaining from others, Parrot, 27, Sticky Hair, 37, Bull, 43, Quails, 55, Desert, 65, Rice, 79, Prince, 127
intelligence,
  using your, Sticky Hair, 37

J
joining in,
  importance of, Quails, 55
joy, (also see happiness),
  dancing for, Goose, 97
  in being with friends, Elephant, 48, Rice, 79, Stag, 103, Lion, 121
  of learning, Sticky Hair, 37, Kingshuk, 59, Prince, 127
  of succeeding, Bull, 43, Desert, 65
judging,
  others fairly, Lion, 121
justness, Stag, 103, Whatnot, 115

K
karma (reaping what you sow – see p.11), Sticky Hair, 37 Quails, 55, Rice, 79, Peacock, 84, Whatnot Fruit, 115
kindness,
  toward others, Parrot, 27, Sticky Hair, 37, Bull, 43, Elephant, 48, Rice, 79, Goblet, 90, Goose, 97, Stag, 103, Monkey, 108, Lion, 121
ksanti (patience and calmness – see p.13), Parrot, 27, Sticky Hair, 37, Quails, 55, Kingshuk, 59, Desert, 65, Stag, 103, Monkey, 108

L

learning,
from others, Quails, 55, Kingshuk, 59, Desert, 65, Rabbit, 74, Rice, 79, Whatnot Fruit, 115, Prince, 127
from your own mistakes, Turtle, 33, Wood Gatherer, 71, Rabbit, 74, Rice, 79, Peacock, 84, Whatnot Fruit, 115, Goblin, 131
importance of, Quails, 55, Kingshuk, 59, Rabbit, 74, Prince, 127

listening,
to inner self, Sticky Hair, 37
to others, Sticky Hair, 37, Bull, 43, Quails, 55, Kingshuk, 59, Rabbit, 74, Whatnot Fruit, 115, Prince, 127, Goblin, 131
to sounds of nature, Desert, 65

love,
enduring nature of, Elephant, 48, Prince, 127
of beauty, Kingshuk, 59, Stag, 103
of fellow creatures, Parrot, 27, Elephant, 48, Quails, 55, Rabbit, 74, Goose, 97, Lion, 121
of family, Lion, 121, Prince, 127
of friends, Parrot, 27, Elephant, 48, Rice, 79, Stag, 103, Lion, 121
of laughter, Elephant, 48

loving-kindness (*see* metta bhavana), Elephant, 48, Rice, 79, Goose, 97, Stag, 103

loyalty,
toward friends, Parrot, 27, Lion, 121, Goblin, 131

M

making the best,
of a situation, Desert, 65, Lion, 121
of what you have, Elephant, 48, Rice, 79

metta bhavana (loving kindness – see pp.12, 136), Elephant, 48, Rice, 79, Goose, 97, Stag, 103

modesty, Monkey, 108

motivation, self-, Parrot, 27, Turtle, 33, Sticky Hair, 37, Quails, 55, Desert, 65, Prince, 127

N

nature,
delight in, Kingshuk, 59

non-violence, Stag, 103, Monkey, 108

O

observation,
of others, Elephant, 48, Quails, 55, Rice, 79, Prince, 127, Goblin, 131

open-mindedness,
about future, Rice, 79, Prince, 127
about others, Kingshuk, 59, Monkey, 108, Lion, 121

optimism, Desert, 65, Lion, 121

P

past,
valuing the, Prince, 127

patience, Kingshuk, 59
with others' behaviour, Monkey, 108
with changing circumstances, Desert, 65

peace,
of mind, Rice, 79
when alone, Monkey, 108

perseverance, Parrot, 27, Sticky Hair, 37, Bull, 43, Desert, 65

planning,
ahead, Turtle, 33, Quails, 55, Rabbit, 74, Prince, 127

pleasure, (*see also* enjoyment)
in doing right thing, Rice, 79, Goblet, 90
in entertainments, Rice, 79
in friendship, Sticky Hair, 37, Elephant, 48, Stag, 103, Lion, 121
in helping others, Elephant, 48, Rabbit, 74, Rice, 79, Goblet, 97, Stag, 103
in laughter, Elephant, 48
in nature, Kingshuk, 59
in solving a problem, Quails, 55, Desert, 65, Stag, 103
in succeeding, Bull, 43, Desert, 65
in the moment, Elephant, 48, Goblet, 90, Prince, 127

positive thinking, Parrot, 27, Desert, 65
about future, Rice, 79, Lion 121, Prince, 127
about others, Monkey, 108
about own capabilities, Sticky Hair, 37

potential, Prince, 127

praise,
of others, Bull, 43

prajna (wisdom – see p.13), Parrot, 27, Sticky Hair, 37, Elephant, 48, Desert, 65, Rabbit, 74, Stag, 103, Monkey, 108, Whatnot Fruit, 115

pride,
in others' achievements, Bull, 43
in own achievements, Desert, 65
in own appearance, Stag, 103
of others in you, Prince, 127

protecting,
others, Parrot, 27, Quails, 55, Desert, 65, Rabbit, 74, Rice, 79, Goose, 97, Stag, 103, Monkey, 108, Whatnot Fruit, 115, Lion, 121, Goblin, 131
yourself, Quails, 55, Desert, 65, Goblin, 131

providing,
for others, Elephant, 48, Wood Gatherer, 71, Rice, 79

R

recognition,
of one's own actions, Bull, 43, Wood Gatherer, 71, Rice, 79, Peacock, 84, Monkey, 108, Whatnot Fruit, 115
of one's own intelligence, Sticky Hair, 37, Prince, 127
of others' achievements, Bull, 43, Rice, 79
of others' feelings, Bull, 43, Elephant, 48, Stag, 103

relationships,
established, Prince, 127
new friends, Sticky Hair, 37, Elephant, 48, Rice, 79, Stag, 103, Lion, 121

respect,
for animals, Stag, 103
for environment, Desert, 65
for experience, Prince, 127
for hard work, Bull, 43
for natural world, Parrot, 27, Lion, 121
for nature, Kingshuk, 59
for others, Parrot, 27, Rice, 79, Stag, 103, Lion, 121, Prince, 127
for others' talents, Prince, 127

responsibility,
of own actions, Sticky Hair, 37, Bull, 43, Wood Gatherer, 71, Rabbit, 74, Whatnot Fruit, 115, Goblin, 131
taking, Quails, 55, Desert, 65,

Rice, 79, Prince, 127

risk-taking,
importance of, Parrot, 27

S

safety,
feelings of, Stag, 103, Lion, 121

self-acceptance, Bull, 43, Rabbit, 74, Rice, 79, Whatnot, 115

self-belief, Parrot, 27, Sticky Hair, 37, Bull, 43, Desert, 65

self-determination, Parrot, 27, Rice, 79

self-development, Bull, 43, Rabbit, 74, Rice, 79, Monkey, 108, Prince, 127

self-discipline, Quails, 55, Rabbit, 74, Whatnot Fruit, 115, Prince, 127

self-esteem, Prince, 127

self-expression, Lion, 121, Prince, 127

self-image, Prince, 127

self-improvement, Sticky Hair, 37, Wood Gatherer, 71, Rice, 79, Peacock, 84, Prince, 127

self-understanding, Sticky Hair, 37, Goblin, 131

selflessness, Parrot, 27, Rabbit, 74, Rice, 79, Stag, 103

sharing,
in others' achievements, Bull, 43
knowledge, Sticky Hair, 37, Kingshuk, 59, Rabbit, 74
Whatnot Fruit, 115, Prince, 127, Goblin, 131
laughter, Elephant, 48, Kingshuk, 59
problems, Quails, 55, Stag, 103, Goblin, 131
talents, Prince, 127
with others, Elephant, 48, Rice, 79, Goblet, 90, Lion, 121

sila (ethical behaviour – see p.13), Elephant, 48, Goblet, 90, Stag, 103, Lion, 121

sociability, Sticky Hair, 37, Rice, 79, Lion, 121

solitude,
enjoyment of, Monkey, 108

strength,
inner, Parrot, 27, Sticky Hair, 37, Bull, 43, Rice, 79, Prince, 127
of character, Parrot, 27, Sticky Hair, 37, Bull, 43, Rice, 79, Stag, 103, Monkey, 108, Prince, 127

sympathy,
  for others, Parrot, 27, Bull, 43,
    Elephant, 48, Rice, 79, Goblet, 90,
    Goose, 97, Stag, 103, Monkey, 108,
    Lion, 121

T

talents,
  sharing with others, Sticky Hair, 37,
    Prince, 127
teamwork, Turtle, 33, Quails, 55,
  Kingshuk, 59, Goblin, 131
temptation,
  resisting, Whatnot Fruit, 115
thankfulness,
  for what you are given, Elephant, 48,
    Rice, 79, Goblet, 90, Goose, 97
  toward others, Parrot, 27,
    Elephant, 48, Rabbit, 74, Rice, 79,
    Goblet, 90, Goose, 97, Stag, 103,
    Monkey, 108, Lion, 121, Prince, 127,
    Goblin, 131
thinking,
  about absent friends and loved ones,
    Prince, 127
  about others, Parrot, 27, Elephant, 48,
    Rice, 79, Whatnot Fruit, 115,
    Lion, 121, Goblin, 131
  independently, Prince, 127
  wholesome, Goblet, 90
thoughtfulness,
  toward others, Parrot, 27, Bull, 43,
    Elephant, 48, Rice, 79, Goblet, 90,
    Goose, 97, Stag, 103, Monkey, 108,
    Lion, 121
tolerance, Bull, 43, Elephant, 48,
  Monkey, 108
trust,
  of others in you, Sticky Hair, 37,
    Goblet, 90, Stag, 103, Lion, 121,
    Goblin, 131
  in others, Sticky Hair, 37, Bull, 43,
    Quails, 55, Rabbit, 74, Stag, 103,
    Lion, 121
  in the future, Lion, 121, Prince, 127
  in yourself, Sticky Hair, 37, Desert, 65,
    Prince, 127

U

understanding,
  of animals and birds, Goose, 97,
    Stag, 103
  of change, Prince, 127

of life's flow, Prince, 127
of need to be afraid sometimes,
  Rabbit, 74
of need to take charge of your life,
  Turtle, 33, Quails, 55, Rice, 79,
  Prince, 127
of others, Bull, 43, Elephant, 48,
  Rice, 79, Stag, 103, Lion, 121
of oneself, Sticky Hair, 37, Bull, 43,
  Rice, 79, Peacock, 84, Prince, 127
of situation, Turtle, 33, Quails, 55,
  Desert, 65, Rabbit, 74, Whatnot
  Fruit, 115, Lion, 121, Goblin, 131

V

virya (effort – see p.13), Parrot, 27,
  Sticky Hair, 37, Bull, 43, Stag, 103

W

wisdom, Parrot, 27, Sticky Hair, 37,
  Elephant, 48, Quails, 55, Desert, 65,
  Rabbit, 74, Stag, 103, Monkey, 108,
  Whatnot Fruit, 115, Prince, 127
working together, Turtle, 33,
  Quails, 55, Kingshuk, 59, Rice, 79,
  Prince, 127

ISSUES

A

absence,
  of friends or family, Elephant, 48,
    Rice, 79, Prince, 127
accusing,
  falsely, Bull, 43
achievement, lack of,
  Wood Gatherer, 71, Rice, 79
aggression, Turtle, 33, Sticky Hair, 37,
  Bull, 43, Rice, 79, Goose, 97
anger, Turtle, 33, Bull, 43, Quails, 55,
  Desert, 65, Goblet, 90, Goose, 97,
  Stag, 103, Monkey, 108
anxiety, (see also fear)
  about being alone, Elephant, 48,
    Rabbit, 74
  about being lost, Desert, 65,
    Rabbit, 74
  about being neglected, Lion, 121
  about frightening situations, Parrot, 27,
    Turtle, 33, Rabbit, 74, Stag, 103,
    Monkey, 108, Lion, 121, Goblin, 131
  about future, Prince, 127

about growing up, Prince, 127
about losing, Bull, 43
about making wrong decision,
  Desert, 65, Wood Gatherer, 71,
  Rabbit, 74, Whatnot Fruit, 115,
  Lion, 121
about new situations, Lion, 121,
  Prince, 127
about separation, Elephant, 48,
  Prince, 127

B

belief, lack of,
  in others, Parrot, 27, Sticky Hair, 37,
    Bull, 43, Kingshuk, 59, Desert, 65,
    Rice, 79, Whatnot Fruit, 115,
    Lion, 121, Goblin, 131
bereavement, Prince, 127
betrayal, Stag, 103, Goblin, 131
bitterness, Lion, 121
blame,
  unfairly, Bull, 43
boasting, Peacock, 84
boredom, Elephant, 48
bragging, Peacock, 84
breaking promises (see promises),
  Turtle, 33, Stag, 103
bullying, Bull, 43

C

callousness, Bull, 43, Rice, 79,
  Goblet, 90, Goose, 97
clumsiness, Peacock, 84
compassion, lack of,
  Bull, 43, Elephant, 48, Rice, 79,
  Goblet, 90, Goose, 97, Stag, 103,
  Monkey, 108
competitiveness, Goblet, 90
concentration, lack of,
  Desert, 65
confidence, lack of,
  in others, Bull, 43, Desert, 65,
  Goblin, 131
conflict, Sticky Hair, 37, Rice, 79,
  Lion, 121
confusion, Parrot, 27, Kingshuk, 59
co-operation, lack of,
  Turtle, 33, Quails, 55, Wood
  Gatherer, 71, Rabbit, 74
criticism, Lion, 121
cruelty,
  toward others, Bull, 43, Rice, 79,
  Goose, 97

D

danger,
  fear of, Parrot, 27, Desert, 65, Rabbit,
    74, Stag, 103, Lion, 121, Goblin, 131
decisions, making bad,
  Quails, 55, Wood Gatherer, 71,
  Rabbit, 74, Goblet, 90, Stag, 103,
  Monkey, 108, Whatnot Fruit, 115
dependence,
  on others for company, Elephant, 48
  on others to help, Rabbit, 74,
    Stag, 103
disappointment,
  in oneself, Wood Gatherer, 71,
    Rabbit, 74, Rice, 79, Peacock, 84
  in others, Bull, 43, Stag, 103, Whatnot
    Fruit, 115
discipline, lack of,
  self, Turtle, 33, Wood Gatherer, 71,
    Rabbit, 74, Whatnot Fruit, 115
dishonesty, Goblet, 90, Stag, 103,
  Whatnot Fruit, 115, Goblin, 131,
dismay,
  feelings of, Stag, 103, Whatnot
    Fruit, 115, Lion, 121, Prince, 127,
    Goblin, 131
dissatisfaction,
  with the way things are, Desert, 65,
    Lion, 121

E

effort, lack of, Wood Gatherer, 71
embarrassment,
  of oneself, Elephant, 48, Rice, 79,
    Peacock, 84
envy,
  of others, Lion, 121
excess,
  indulging in, Rice, 79, Goblet, 90,
    Goose, 97, Stag, 103, Whatnot, 115,
    Goblin, 131

F

faith, lack of,
  in others, Parrot, 27, Bull, 43, Stag,
    103, Whatnot Fruit, 115, Goblin, 131
fear, (see also anxiety)
  of being alone, Rabbit, 74
  of being lost, Desert, 65, Rabbit, 74
  of change, Prince, 127,
  of danger ahead, Parrot, 27,
    Desert, 65, Rabbit, 74, Stag, 103,
    Monkey, 108, Whatnot Fruit, 115,

Lion, 121, Goblin, 131
of failure, Bull, 43, Wood Gatherer, 71
of feeling small in a big world, Desert, 65
of future, Turtle, 33, Lion, 121, Prince, 127
of loss, Prince, 127
of new situations, Desert, 65, Prince, 127
of unknown, Whatnot Fruit, 115, Prince, 127
frustration,
at being laughed at or ridiculed, Turtle, 33, Peacock, 84
at others' behaviour, Monkey, 108, Whatnot Fruit, 115

G
giving up, too easily, Desert, 65, Wood Gatherer, 71
greed, Bull, 43, Elephant, 48, Rice, 79, Goblet, 90, Goose, 97, Stag, 103
grief, Elephant, 48, Rice, 79, Stag, 103, Lion, 121
guilt, lack of, Goblet, 90, Goose, 97, Stag, 103

H
harming, Bull, 43, Goose, 97
helplessness, sense of, Desert, 65, Rabbit, 74
honesty, lack of, Goblet, 90, Stag, 103, Whatnot Fruit, 115

I
ignorance, Peacock, 84, Monkey, 108, Whatnot Fruit, 115, Goblin, 131
immodesty, Peacock, 84
impatience, of others, Bull, 43
impermanence, of life, Prince, 127
indifference, toward others, Rice, 79, Goblet, 90, Goose, 97, Stag, 103, Monkey, 108, Lion, 121
insecurity, in change, Prince, 127

insulting, others, Bull, 43
intolerance,
of allowing others to help, Rabbit, 74
of others, Bull, 43, Quails, 55, Rice, 79, Goose, 97, Lion, 121
isolation, Sticky Hair, 37, Elephant, 48, Rabbit, 74, Rice, 79, Goose, 97, Lion, 121

J
jealousy, Lion, 121
judging, Turtle, 33, Bull, 43, Rice, 79, Lion, 121

L
laziness, Elephant, 48, Wood Gatherer, 71
listening, lack of, Rabbit, 74, Rice, 79, Whatnot Fruit, 115, Goblin, 131
loneliness, Elephant, 48, Rabbit, 74, Rice, 79, Lion, 121
loss, Elephant, 48, Prince, 127
loyalty, lack of, Stag, 103
lying, Goblet, 90

M
meanness, Rice, 79, Goblet, 90, Goose, 97, Monkey, 108
mistreating, Bull, 43, Rice, 79, Goose, 97, Whatnot, 115
mistrust, of others, Sticky Hair, 37, Stag, 103, Goblin, 131
motivation, lack of, Wood Gatherer, 71

N
negative thinking, about others, Bull, 43, Lion, 121, Prince, 127
neglect, of others, Rice, 79, Goose, 97

O
overdependence, on others, Lion, 121, Prince, 127

P
pessimism, Parrot, 27, Desert, 65, Lion, 121
possessiveness, Rice, 79, Goblet, 90
promises, breaking, Turtle, 33, Stag, 103
not honouring, Stag, 103

Q
quarrelling, Quails, 55

R
regret,
at losing someone, Elephant, 48, Prince, 127
at one's own actions, Bull, 43, Wood Gatherer, 71, Rabbit, 74, Rice, 79, Peacock, 84, Monkey, 108, Whatnot Fruit, 115
lack of, Goose, 97, Stag, 103, Monkey, 108
resentment, Turtle, 33, Bull, 43, Goblet, 90, Lion, 121
respect, lack of, Bull, 43, Rabbit, 74, Monkey, 108
ridiculing, Turtle, 33
rivalry, Goblet, 90, Lion, 121

S
sadness, Elephant, 48, Goose, 97, Stag, 103, Prince, 127
selfishness, Bull, 43, Rice, 79
separation anxiety, Elephant, 48, Lion, 121, Prince, 127
shame, lack of, Goblet, 90, Goose, 97, Stag, 103
in oneself, Rice, 79, Peacock, 84, Whatnot Fruit, 115, Lion, 121
showing off, Peacock, 84
slyness, Goblet, 90, Goose, 97, Whatnot Fruit, 115
smugness, Peacock, 84
spitefulness, Elephant, 48, Rice, 79, Goblet, 90, Goose, 97

sorrow, Rice, 79, Goose, 97, Stag, 103, Lion, 121, Prince, 127
stealing, Whatnot Fruit, 115
stupidity, Turtle, 33, Elephant, 48, Quails, 55, Rabbit, 74, Peacock, 84, Monkey, 108, Whatnot Fruit, 115
suffering,
causing others, Bull, 43, Goose, 97
sympathy, lack of, Bull, 43, Goose, 97, Monkey, 108

T
temptation, giving into, Bull, 43, Elephant, 48, Desert, 65, Wood Gatherer, 71, Rice, 79, Goblet, 90, Goose, 97, Stag, 103, Whatnot Fruit, 115, Goblin, 131
thoughtlessness, Turtle, 33, Bull, 43, Elephant, 48, Wood Gatherer, 71, Rabbit, 74, Rice, 79, Goose, 97, Stag, 103, Monkey, 108, Lion, 121
trust, lack of, Bull, 43, Elephant, 65, Stag, 103, Lion, 121

U
understanding, lack of, Turtle, 33, Bull, 43, Rice, 79, Goose, 97, Stag, 103, Monkey, 108, Lion, 121
unhappiness, Goose, 97, Stag, 103, Lion, 121
unkindness, Bull, 43, Elephant, 48, Rice, 79, Goblet, 90, Goose, 97, Stag, 103, Monkey, 108, Whatnot Fruit, 115, Lion, 121

V
vanity, Peacock, 84

W
wisdom, lack of, Turtle, 33, Elephant, 48, Quails, 55, Wood Gatherer, 71, Rabbit, 74, Monkey, 108
worry, see anxiety

Note from the Author

If anything in this book is inaccurate or misleading, I ask forgiveness of my teachers and of the readers for having unwittingly impeded their way. As for what is accurate, I hope the reader can use it, so that they may attain the truth to which it points.